HER SECRET LEGACY

When one door closes another door opens. Megan had always believed the old saying but nothing could have prepared her for the surprises that lay in store when her life took an unexpected and mysterious turn. Faced with the secrets of the past, Megan uncovered one clue after another but became increasingly unsure just who she could trust.

MARGARET McDONAGH

———————◆———————

HER SECRET LEGACY

Complete and Unabridged

LINFORD
Leicester

First published in Great Britain in 2004

First Linford Edition
published 2004

British Library CIP Data

McDonagh, Margaret
   Her secret legacy.—Large print ed.—
Linford romance library
   1. Love stories
   2. Large type books
   I. Title
   823.9'14 [F]

   ISBN 1–84395–534–2

Published by
F. A. Thorpe (Publishing)
Anstey, Leicestershire

Set by Words & Graphics Ltd.
Anstey, Leicestershire
Printed and bound in Great Britain by
T. J. International Ltd., Padstow, Cornwall

This book is printed on acid-free paper

1

'What you need,' Helen King announced as she swept a cherry-red gloss across her lips, 'is a hot new job, and a hot new man!'

Typical Helen! Megan Fitzgerald sprawled across the bed in her friend's room and propped her chin in her hands. She agreed about the job, Megan admitted with a wry smile, but not about the man. As far as she was concerned the male of the species was a no-go area from now on.

She smothered a sigh and watched as Helen applied the finishing touches to her make-up, her mind reflecting on the turbulent events of the last week.

'How can anyone lose a job, a flat and a boyfriend in under seven days?' she pondered aloud.

Helen grinned.

'Nothing you do surprises me!'

'Thanks. Well, somehow I've managed it.'

'The job wasn't your fault. There was no inkling at all that the company would go under, was there?'

'Far from it,' Megan agreed.

The computer firm she had worked for these last five years, since university, had seemed go ahead and successful. It had come as a huge shock when it had collapsed almost overnight, calling in the receivers and consigning the entire staff to the ranks of the unemployed.

'Whether any of us will receive a penny of the back pay we are owed looks increasingly unlikely,' Megan admitted morosely, thinking of the sorry state of her finances.

This brought her to the second loss — her flat. Well, it was more of a bedsit, really, but whatever she called it, she was unable to pay the rent, and the landlord, not renowned for an understanding nature, was unprepared to extend her the time until she found another job.

'I still think it was a bit much chucking you out of your flat like that,' Helen commented, fixing in a pair of stylish gold earrings.

'Mr Samuels was right when he said it was in the terms of my rental agreement, but even I didn't think he would be quite so strict. He told me he had a business to run and there were plenty of people with ready money on his waiting list!'

'A waiting list, for his flats?' Helen snorted in disbelief. 'Pull the other one!'

Smiling, Megan had to agree that it sounded far-fetched, but whatever the reasons, she was here, belongings in tow, back in the sanctuary of the two-bedroomed loft she and Helen had shared after arriving in London fresh from university. After Megan had moved out to be nearer her work, Helen had kept the place on.

Megan rolled on to her side and picked a stray piece of fluff from the leg of her jeans.

'Thanks for letting me move back in here at such short notice.'

'I would have been furious if you had thought of going anywhere else.'

A sparkle of mischief appeared in Helen's powder-blue eyes as she swung round from the dressing table, dabbing a musky perfume behind her ears.

'I can't tell you how much I've missed having you here.'

'We did have some laughs, didn't we? Really good times.'

'And we will again. I only wish it could begin tonight. I could always cancel my date.'

'Don't be daft! You've been looking forward to this concert for ages,' Megan protested. 'You haven't stopped talking about the dishy Matt Halloran since he joined your bank two months ago.'

A grin dimpled Helen's cheeks as she crossed to her wardrobe.

'I know. I couldn't believe it when he told me he'd got these tickets and asked me to go with him.'

'And you think I'm about to let you

4

pass up the opportunity of being squired off to Wembley Arena by your dream man?' Megan teased, smiling at the blush of excitement that warmed Helen's delicate, fine-boned face.

'OK, you've made your point.'

The early-evening light that filtered through the windows made Helen's short ash-blonde hair appear silvery white, Megan thought, reflecting on the total contrasts in their looks. Whereas Helen was petite and slender, she herself was several inches taller and her own frame could only be described as curvy. Her hair was almost shoulder-length, rich chestnut, framing her face and accentuating her slanting hazel eyes.

'Can you zip me up?'

Squirming to the edge of the bed, Megan fastened Helen's sequined black dress.

'You look fabulous. Matt won't be able to resist you.'

'Splendid!'

A car horn sounded down on the

street, and with a cry of nervous excitement, Helen dashed to the window and looked out.

'It's Matt!'

She spun back into the room, frantically searching for her bag and shoes.

'Are you sure I look OK?'

Megan laughed, unaccustomed to seeing her friend so flustered.

'Positive. Have you got everything?'

'I think so. Matt's got the tickets.'

After Helen had double-checked her appearance and the contents of her bag, Megan followed her to the front door.

'I feel as nervous as a teenager,' Helen admitted with a self-conscious smile.

'Take a deep breath. You're a sophisticated, beautiful and successful woman. Matt's a lucky man.'

Helen beamed before her eyes clouded once more.

'I hate to go out and leave you on your first night back. Are you sure you'll be OK?'

'I'll be fine,' Megan assured for the countless time, opening the door. 'Have a wonderful time!'

'I won't do anything you wouldn't!'

Smiling as Helen's parting words floated back up the stairway, Megan closed the door. After making herself a sandwich and a cup of tea, she went through to the spare room to make a start on sorting out the boxes and bags of her belongings that had been packed in a hurried, slapdash fashion. Her task completed, she had a long, relaxing bath then tumbled into bed for an early night.

Once there, she found she couldn't sleep. Her thoughts turned unwillingly to the third loss of the week — Stuart Crawley. They had been going out together for seven months, but the fun and excitement that had marked the beginning of their relationship had deteriorated over the weeks, with Stuart becoming more and more controlling.

In her heart of hearts, Megan wasn't shedding any tears at the break-up. She was just annoyed that in hindsight she had surrendered so much of her independence to Stuart. At least Helen, who had hated him on sight, hadn't said, 'I told you so' too often.

Under his suave exterior, Stuart had possessed a very unpleasant dark streak to his character. She knew she was well out of the relationship but it still smarted. Coming when it did, the unpleasantness between them at their acrimonious break-up was the final straw, an unsettling conclusion to a rotten week.

One thing was for sure. She was in no hurry to start another relationship, no matter what Helen said about finding a new man. She was equally determined not to dwell on her current situation. It would be all too easy to waste time worrying and finding herself stuck in a rut. That was not in her nature. Instead, she looked forward, positively.

The changes happening in her professional and personal lives were gateways to new opportunities. One of them would open, she told herself. When it did, she would be ready to walk through it.

★ ★ ★

'Hard at it, Luke?'

Glancing up from his task of restoring order to the rambling rose that intermingled with the profusion of honeysuckle that gave the empty cottage its name, Luke Warrender saw the village postman leaning on the gate, his red van on the grassy verge, the engine idling.

'Hello, Bob,' he greeted, standing to stretch tired muscles.

'Good to see you bringing some colour back to the old place.'

'I thought it was time.'

The older man nodded sadly.

'Reckon it is. We all miss Sophie.'

'Yes.'

'It's to be sold is it, the cottage?' the postman probed with customary interest.

'I don't know.'

Luke averted his gaze. Actually, he did know. He'd been privy to Sophie's secrets, and to her wishes, but he kept her confidence. He wondered what was happening to date about the cottage. Was the solicitor any closer to fulfilling the terms of Sophie's will?

'I don't recall Sophie having any relatives.'

Luke shrugged non-committally at the postman, determined not to be drawn and have gossip spread around the district. Disappointed by the silence, Bob pushed himself away from the gate.

'Well, I'd best get on. Nice talking with you.'

''Bye, Bob.'

As the van left the lane and the engine sound faded in the distance, Luke sighed and surveyed the front of Honeysuckle Cottage. Nestling as it did in the shelter of the trees on the outskirts of the sleepy Sussex village, it was pretty, with its whitewashed walls and large, secluded garden. Luke ran a work-roughened hand across his jaw, his flint grey eyes hardening as he frowned.

He knew the villagers were curious about the cottage, and about him, but whatever the legal state of things, he was determined to keep the place in order as he had promised Sophie.

He swallowed the sudden constriction in his throat. Sophie had never let him down in life. He would not let her down in death. Only time would tell what changes were to come and what the future held in store.

2

Megan sat at the breakfast counter in the compact kitchen of Helen's flat and sipped her coffee.

Since becoming jobless ten days ago, she had scanned the situations vacant columns and applied for several possible openings. Already she had a couple of interviews arranged for the following week. With her experience and references she was not unduly worried, not yet, but her depleted finances could not be ignored indefinitely, and she had not closed her mind to the possibility of broadening the scope of her applications.

Reaching out for an apple from the well-stocked fruit bowl, she smiled as Helen came into the room and dropped a stack of mail on the counter top.

' 'Morning,' she greeted, her smile widening to a grin at the rosy glow on her friend's face. 'I gather you and Matt enjoyed your dinner date last night?'

Helen's cheeks warmed still further.

'We did!'

In the days since the concert, her friend had seen Matt every minute she could. Megan was delighted for their happiness but was beginning to feel in the way. For all their friendship, she knew that both Helen and herself had reached the stage in their lives when they needed their own space. Sharing the flat again had to be a temporary measure. As soon as she had fixed up a new job, it would be time to move on and put the pieces of her life back together.

'You've got some re-directed letters,' Helen announced, slipping on the jacket of her bank uniform. 'Anything interesting?'

Megan flicked absently through the envelopes.

'I doubt it. Bills mostly, and junk mail. Hold on. What's this?'

'It looks rather formal and official,'

Helen remarked, peering over her shoulder.

While Helen poured herself some coffee, Megan slit the envelope open and pulled out a brief but concise letter typed on posh, headed paper.

'It's from a firm of solicitors,' she murmured, her eyes widening as she scanned the contents of the letter. 'Good heavens!'

'What is it?'

'I don't believe it! Apparently I'm the beneficiary of a will.'

'Never!'

Helen laughed, setting down her mug and taking the letter Megan held out to her, eyebrows rising in bemusement.

'Who on earth is Sophie Unsworth?'

Megan frowned in confusion.

'I have no idea.'

'I didn't know you had an aunt.'

'Neither did I,' Megan agreed, her puzzlement deepening. 'I've no family at all.'

'Well, these people seem to have gone to great lengths to find you,' Helen pointed out, passing back the letter.

'There must be some mistake.'

'You won't know until you call them. I wonder what she's left you!'

Megan wondered, too. Intrigued by the mystery, she examined the address. Kaye, Herman and Wells, she read, solicitors in Brighton.

'I'll ring later this morning and find out.'

'I have to be off,' Helen said, gathering her things together. 'I shall expect a full report when I get home tonight.'

Smiling as the door closed behind her friend, Megan went to have a shower. As she shampooed her hair she pondered on the unexpected letter and the unlikely possibility of a relative she had never known existed. By ten o'clock, dressed in a cool, sleeveless dress, Megan sat cross-legged on the sofa, the letter by her side. Picking up the cordless phone she tapped out the Brighton number, drumming her fingers as she waited for the connection.

'Kaye, Herman and Wells,' a stiff and formal female voice announced. 'How may I help you?'

Megan glanced down at the letter.

'I would like to speak with Mr Jeremy Kaye.'

'Your name, please?'

Megan gave it, then her fingers resumed their idle drumming as a pleasant melody sounded in her ear. The tune ended and a gravelly, male voice came on the line.

'Miss Fitzgerald, I'm Jeremy Kaye. Thank you for responding to my letter.'

'I apologise for the delay, but I have recently moved and your letter was re-directed from my old address,' she informed him. 'Frankly, Mr Kaye, I'm confused and intrigued.'

'Yes, quite so. Well, now . . . '

There was a pause and Megan heard papers being rustled.

'When can you come and see me, Miss Fitzgerald?'

Surprised at the request, Megan hesitated.

'Are you sure this really concerns me? As far as I know I am not related to your client.'

'Let me see. Here we are, Miss Fitzgerald,' the solicitor continued.

He then began rattling off the names of her late parents and the grandparents she had never known.

He even had her date and place of birth and the school she had attended.

'Is that information correct?'

'Yes. Yes, it is,' she confirmed, more puzzled than ever.

'Splendid. Then it would seem that you are indeed the young lady I have been searching for.'

Megan took a couple of moments to gather her scattered thoughts.

'So what exactly is the position, Mr Kaye?' she asked at length. 'Your letter implied I was to inherit something, but what?'

'I would prefer not to discuss the details over the telephone, if you don't mind. A visit here to my office would be in order, if you can arrange it.'

'Yes, if you think it is necessary,' she consented with a frown.

'Good. When would be convenient?'

As she was a lady of leisure at the moment there was no time like the present, Megan decided.

'I have a few days free, Mr Kaye.'

'Splendid! How about tomorrow?' he suggested. 'Could you come to my office about four o'clock? We'll arrange accommodation for you.'

'Accommodation?' Megan exclaimed.

'There is quite a bit of business to attend to, Miss Fitzgerald. We can discuss matters tomorrow afternoon, then I will have the following morning free should you wish to take things further.'

'I see,' she murmured, not seeing at all.

Wondering just what 'things' the solicitor was referring to, Megan agreed to the appointment and disconnected the call. Sitting back on the sofa, she expelled a deep breath. Goodness! The man certainly knew how to arouse a person's curiosity!

* * *

The telephone was ringing when Luke arrived home after visiting a client in a neighbouring village. Dropping his notebook on his cluttered desk, he picked up the receiver before the answering machine kicked in.

'Luke Warrender.'

'Hello, it's Mr Kaye. I have some good news for you.'

'You've located Megan Fitzgerald?' he queried, leaning against the desk.

'Better than that. I have just spoken with her on the telephone and she is coming to see me tomorrow afternoon. I plan to show her the cottage the following morning. Are things in order there?'

'Yes, I've been working in the garden in my spare time.'

'Excellent, thank you. I'm sure Sophie would appreciate all you have done.'

Luke's jaw tightened but he made no comment. Moving round his desk, he checked his appointment diary. It would take a bit of juggling round, but . . .

'I'll have a couple of hours free that morning. Perhaps I could join you at the cottage,' he suggested, his tone calm and controlled.

'Of course. It would be an excellent idea for you and Miss Fitzgerald to meet as soon as possible.'

After hanging up the phone, Luke sat on his swivel chair and gazed out of the window at the ridge of the South Downs. So, she would soon be here. Now it was real and he wasn't at all sure how he felt about it. A plaintive miaow impinged on his consciousness, then sharp claws pierced his jeans, grazing his thighs as his cat stole sinuously on to his lap.

'Ouch!' he complained, allowing the cat to snuggle against him. 'Your claws are lethal weapons, Tugga.'

He absently ran his fingers through

the silken, tortoiseshell fur, feeling the rumble as Tugga purred with contentment. Rising to his feet, he carried her through to the kitchen.

'You want some lunch, girl?' he murmured, setting her on the floor to wrap impatiently round his legs while he measured out some food.

He returned to his study, making some calls to re-schedule his work for the next couple of days. That done, he tried to concentrate on roughing out some preliminary designs for revamping the garden he had just visited. Instead, he found himself unable to set his mind free. In two days, Megan Fitzgerald would arrive. Whether she would live up to Sophie's expectations was another matter entirely.

3

Megan's sense of anticipation was high as her train pulled out of Victoria Station the next afternoon. Since her conversation with the solicitor, her mind had been buzzing with the ramifications, but she was no closer to discovering who the mysterious Aunt Sophie was, or guessing what she might have left her.

'I wish I could come with you,' Helen had exclaimed on hearing the latest news. 'It is so exciting!'

'It will probably all turn out to be a lot of fuss over nothing,' Megan had predicted.

Agog at the possibilities, Helen had fired questions in rapid succession, but Megan had no answers. She only wished she did. The wait was frustrating and tantalising, but she was trying not to have unrealistic expectations.

'It's more than likely that despite Mr Kaye's assurances, some mistake has been made,' she had pointed out to Helen, dampening further enthusiasm. 'Either that or whatever trinket has been bequeathed to me will be as unexciting as it is unexpected.'

'So why would he insist you stay the night in Brighton?' her friend had persisted over breakfast that morning. 'What is it you may wish to take further, as he says?'

Sighing at the futility of the speculation, Megan now tried to put all thoughts of what lay ahead from her mind and took her new CHRISTNA JONES novel from her bag, losing herself in the warm, enjoyable world of the assorted characters.

The train pulled in at Brighton Station within an hour of leaving London. Megan walked along the platform, crossed the concourse and went outside to stand a moment to collect her bearings in the early summer warmth.

With time on her hands before her appointment, she walked down the long hill towards the seafront. The sun was strong and there was a tang in the air, a saltiness that was foreign to her after the city. Crossing the busy coast road, she wandered along the promenade between the two piers before leaning on the railings and looking down at the shingle beach where the gently-swelling ripples lapped as the sea turned at high tide.

Despite the sunshine and the clear sea air filling her lungs, Megan turned in the direction of the town. Impatience denied her any pleasure in her break beside the sea. Unsure of her destination, she decided to take a taxi to the offices of Kaye, Herman and Wells. Housed in a terraced building, the firm occupied the two lower floors. It was tastefully decorated if a touch bland and old-fashioned, Megan decided, as she crossed the reception area and gave her name to the severe-looking woman who sat behind a desk.

'Mr Kaye is expecting you,' the older woman informed her with the ghost of a smile. 'I'll show you straight in.'

Smoothing down the skirt of her smart red linen suit, Megan followed up a flight of stairs and along a carpeted corridor. The woman stopped and rapped on an unmarked door.

As they entered, the first thing Megan discovered was that Mr Kaye was nothing like the image she had formed of him from his voice. Surprised, she found him to be a few years beyond retirement age, an unfailingly courteous man with grey hair, kindly brown eyes and a heavily-wrinkled face. Dressed in a crumpled, old-fashioned suit, he rose from behind a vast, leather-topped desk stacked high with files and assorted papers, and took her hand in both of his. His skin was warm and papery, but his grip was firm.

'I am delighted to meet you, Miss Fitzgerald. Thank you so much for coming today. Please, sit down,' he invited cordially, directing her to a comfortable, if battered, wing chair. 'May I offer you tea?'

Charmed, Megan smiled.

'Tea would be lovely, thank you.'

'Could you organise that, please, Mrs Davies?'

The task under way, Mr Kaye engaged her in small talk, setting her at ease until the tea tray arrived. Megan looked at the china teapot, cups, saucers, milk jug, sugar and plate of shortbread, and swallowed down a nervous giggle at the quaintness of it all.

When Mrs Davies left, closing the office door, leaving them in privacy, Megan sipped her tea and watched as Mr Kaye opened a file and rummaged through the papers. He glanced up and smiled as he fixed a pair of reading glasses somewhat precariously on the bridge of his nose.

'Now, I expect you are keen to know the details of why you are here.'

'Very much so,' Megan admitted, nerves knotting in her stomach. 'I still cannot believe I am the right person. To my knowledge I didn't have an aunt.'

Mr Kaye had another rummage in the file.

'Perhaps I should first explain your relationship to Sophie Unsworth. Do you know much about your family history?'

'Very little. My father was killed in a car accident when I was ten,' she explained, frowning as she recalled dim memories of the man who was rarely at home, his work as a sales rep taking him all over the country. 'My mother passed away shortly after I started university.'

The factual statement spoke little of their difficult relationship, Megan reflected. Forty when Megan had been born, her mother had been a distant woman, not given to confidences and open displays of affection.

'I always assumed I had no other family,' she continued now, banishing her difficult memories. 'No relatives were ever mentioned, and there was no indication of anything to the contrary amongst my mother's things.'

'I see,' Mr Kaye said and cleared his throat. 'It is my understanding that your maternal grandparents were divorced, much more frowned upon in those days, of course. Your grandfather was rumoured to be a difficult man, very strong-willed. He remarried, to the disapproval of the family, and they cut him off, but he had a late child, Sophie.'

'I had no idea,' Megan murmured, her mind racing.

'Quite so.'

Adjusting his glasses, the solicitor continued.

'Forgive me, Miss Fitzgerald, but you are twenty-six this year, I believe.'

'That's right.'

'Sophie was only ten years older than you. I have a photograph of her if you wish to see it.'

'Yes, please.'

While he searched for the print,

Megan struggled to grasp all she had been told. She realised now she had envisaged the mysterious aunt, if she existed at all, as an older woman, someone of her mother's generation.

'Here we are!'

Megan took the picture Mr Kaye passed to her. The smiling, vivacious woman who stared back at her was a complete surprise. Although her own hair was a vibrant chestnut, her eyes hazel, and Sophie had been dark with ebony hair and green eyes, they were very alike in features and bone structure. Megan stared at the face in shock.

She felt equally taken aback by the sudden, inner knowledge she experienced that had they met, she and Sophie would have liked each other, would have talked and laughed together.

'You can be in no doubt now about the connection between you, Miss Fitzgerald.'

Giving herself a mental shake, Megan

turned her attention back to the kindly man who waited patiently for her reaction.

'No,' she allowed, still struggling to accept the reality. 'Clearly Sophie must have known about me.'

'My understanding is that she only discovered the information recently. She became ill shortly after she instigated the search for you. It made her all the more determined you should meet. Sadly we were unable to track you down in time.'

As he went on to explain the circumstances, Megan looked back at the photograph. Sophie appeared to have been such an alive and happy woman. It was tragic she had died so young. Megan felt a real surge of grief that the search had been successful only after Sophie had succumbed to her illness. She wished wholeheartedly she had had the chance to know her.

'Perhaps we should turn our attention to the inheritance itself.'

Megan nodded her consent to Mr

Kaye's suggestion, unable to comprehend that Sophie had left her anything, or why.

'Good, good. Now then, Sophie had no husband or children, and as far as we have been able to ascertain, you are now the last of your family. You became very important to Sophie, Miss Fitzgerald. She told me more than once that she felt strangely close to you, even though you had never met.'

Megan felt a prickle of shock as the solicitor's words mirrored her own earlier instinctive thoughts.

'The instructions in Sophie's will are very detailed,' Mr Kaye continued. 'She was most adamant about what she wanted. In that respect she was very much her father's daughter — stubborn and single-minded once she had decided on a course of action!'

'But why should she leave anything to me?'

'She wished to right family wrongs. That is what she told me on several occasions.'

As Mr Kaye drew an official document from the file, Megan held her breath.

'We come, then, to the will. It is my duty and my pleasure to inform you that aside from small bequests to her many friends, your aunt, Sophie Unsworth, has left the remainder of her not inconsiderable estate to you, Miss Fitzgerald.'

4

'I can't believe it,' Megan protested, her voice strained as she stared at Mr Kaye, stunned by what he had told her. 'I thought maybe Sophie had left me a piece of furniture or some family items, but this?'

'It's a shock to you, I know, but the fact remains, you are the main beneficiary of Sophie's will.'

Bemused, her tea forgotten, Megan clasped her hands in her lap to halt their shaking.

'What exactly does Sophie's estate entail?'

'I'll list the details for you, and then you can ask me any questions. How does that sound?' Mr Kaye suggested kindly.

'Fine, thank you.'

Gathering her scattered wits, Megan concentrated with mounting incredulity as the solicitor adjusted his glasses once more and read from the will.

'Aside from the personal bequests to friends, there is some ongoing income from her work. Sophie was a journalist of some repute. She wrote a couple of successful biographies, the rights to which she has left to charity. The rest of the estate is yours.'

'And what does that comprise of?' Megan whispered, pressing a hand to her throat, still unable to absorb the shock.

'There is Sophie's home in one of the downland villages some miles from town, plus the remaining contents. There is her car, of course, and a sum of money from savings and investments, the balance of which will be due to you after probate. After taxes that should amount to something like, let me see.'

He paused, checking his calculations and naming a figure that made Megan gasp. Sitting back in her chair, she gripped the arms for support. There had to be some mistake! Surely Mr

Kaye had not really said what she thought he had. He was talking tens of thousands of pounds, plus a cottage and a car!

'Miss Fitzgerald?'

Glancing up, she realised Mr Kaye was watching her with concern.

'I'm sorry, I . . . '

'Not at all, my dear. Is there anything you are unclear about?'

'Why? Why would Sophie leave all this to me?'

'I can only repeat what I explained to you before.'

Mr Kaye's brow furrowed, and he leaned forward, steepling his hands under his chin.

'Sophie was a client of mine for many years, a charming person, successful, loyal, very stubborn,' he informed with a reminiscent and affectionate smile. 'She was very sure about what she wanted.'

'I still find it hard to understand.'

'As I told you, Sophie was insistent that she right family wrongs.'

'But what would have happened if you had not found me?'

'I have quite detailed instructions to carry out in respect of the estate. Other arrangements would have been in place should circumstances have dictated that you were unable to inherit.'

'I see.'

Smiling, Mr Kaye began to gather together his papers and put them back in the file.

'You'll have time to absorb what has happened. For now I suggest that you simply enjoy your good fortune.'

'Thank you. I didn't mean to sound ungracious. It is all so unexpected, such a shock, not only the inheritance, but learning I had other family I never knew about.'

'I understand,' he admitted, his smile kindly. 'Now then, I shall organise for you to be taken to the hotel. My wife and I would be delighted if you would have dinner with us in the restaurant this evening.'

'That would be lovely.'

'Splendid! Then, in the morning, we can pay a visit to Sophie's cottage, your cottage, Miss Fitzgerald,' he added heartily.

Rising to his feet, he escorted her downstairs to reception.

'Mrs Davies will organise a car for you, my dear, and my wife and I will meet you at the hotel at seven thirty, if that is agreeable?'

Megan confirmed that it was, and within a short time found herself in a luxurious, seafront hotel, ensconced in a large, comfortable room. She sank down on the double bed. Was she dreaming or had this afternoon actually happened?

Forcing herself into action, she crossed to the window and looked out at the view of the English Channel sparkling under the late afternoon sun. She had anticipated there were to be changes in her life, but had never envisaged anything like this!

After showering, she rang Helen, scarcely believing the news even as she related it to her friend. Helen was beside herself with excitement and Megan laughed, some of her inner tension uncoiling.

'But why did you have to stay down there overnight?' Helen demanded in frustration.

'Mr Kaye and his wife are taking me to dinner. It seemed churlish to refuse,' she answered, lying face down on the bed, wrapped in a fluffy towel. 'Perhaps I shall find out more about Sophie. Anyway,' she continued, twisting the phone cord through her fingers, 'Mr Kaye is showing me the cottage tomorrow morning, so I'll be able to give you a full report when I get back.'

'I can't wait!'

Laughing, Megan hung up and prepared for dinner.

* * *

Sunlight streamed through the window when Megan woke just before eight the next morning. She rolled over, stretching in the comfortable bed. Today she would see Sophie's cottage — her cottage. The very idea of it turned her mind once more to the legacy the unknown Sophie had bequeathed to her. She still found it hard to contemplate such a large sum of money.

All her life she had struggled to make ends meet, putting herself through university, then working hard and living carefully to pay off her student loan. Now she would be able to clear the last hefty chunk of it in one stroke, and see her bank balance in the black for a change!

It would certainly give her a comfortable cushion while she decided what she wanted to do, Megan admitted. Thanks to Sophie's generosity, whole new avenues had been opened up for her. For once she would have the luxury of taking her time, standing back and making choices before jumping at the first job that came her way.

As she prepared for the day ahead,

she pondered further on the cottage. Could she, a city girl, ever contemplate living in a country village, or should she sell it and buy a place of her own back in London?

Her thoughts wandered on as she dressed in a sleeveless, button-through dress in yellow with turquoise flowers which flattered her figure and colouring. Megan slipped her feet into comfortable shoes, picked up her bag and went downstairs.

She had just finished a light breakfast when Mr Kaye arrived to collect her.

'Thank you again for dinner last night,' she offered. 'I had a really nice time.'

'Most enjoyable,' Mr Kaye agreed, ushering her out to his car.

It had not been her usual kind of evening out, Megan admitted to herself as she fastened her seat belt and waited for their journey to begin, nor her usual kind of company. But Louisa Kaye had proved to be a spritely and humorous woman, and the elderly couple had been entertaining and engaging. She hadn't learned much more about Sophie, however, and Megan hoped the day would bring more answers to her many questions.

She relaxed as Mr Kaye drove through the town. The day was balmy, and once they had left Brighton behind, the scenery was pleasant. Mr Kaye asked few questions, speaking only to point out things he believed might interest her, and to tell her a little about the village where the cottage was situated.

Nestling between green fields within the protective arm of the ridge of the South Downs, the village was picturesque, she discovered.

'It is well serviced, with a post office, local shop and a junior school,' Mr Kaye informed her, 'plus the pub, of course.'

The latter was set back from the road. The village houses, some of them large and attractive, appeared well cared for, the gardens lush with shrubs and colourful plants. A small village pond occupied a corner of the green just beyond the pub, where a couple of mothers with toddlers scattered bread for a cluster of greedy ducks.

'Almost here,' Mr Kaye said as they passed the village church and he turned the car down a narrow lane. After another half a mile or so he turned into a gravel drive between two sturdy gateposts. The name Honeysuckle Cottage was embossed on an oval iron plate and fixed in the centre of an open, five-barred gate.

'This is it, my dear. Your cottage.'

Megan's first sight of Honeysuckle Cottage mesmerised her.

Sheltered by a thick wood to the north, and with views of the Downs to the south, the cottage basked serenely in the summer sunshine. A two-storey building, it had white-washed, creeper-clad walls under an old-fashioned stone roof, and it was larger and more beautiful than Megan had ever imagined.

'What do you think?' Mr Kaye queried, watching the play of expressions cross her face.

'It's lovely.'

A free-standing garage stood at the end of the short driveway. The doors were closed, but a small white van stood outside. Was this the vehicle she had inherited? She smothered down a brief and unreasonable flash of disappointment, but as if sensing her thoughts, Mr Kaye smiled.

'The van belongs to Mr Warrender. He's been maintaining order in the garden and keeping a watch on things around the cottage.'

Nodding her understanding and masking her relief, Megan stepped out of the car. The thick, wild hedgerows that bordered the property and sheltered it from view seemed alive with wild flowers. The scents of jasmine and honeysuckle lingered in the warm air, tantalising her as she turned slowly, surveying her surroundings.

'It's so peaceful,' she murmured.

No traffic noise or human hustle and bustle intruded. The only sounds were of birds and bees and the gentle rustle from the trees. Megan, used to a hectic life in London, was surprised to find herself so charmed.

'I expect you would like to look round the house,' Mr Kay suggested, directing her towards the sturdy front door, painted bright red.

Mr Kaye unlocked the door which swung open with the faintest squeak from the hinges. Megan stepped inside, finding herself in a small hallway. The interior was musty, the cottage having been closed for so long, but clearly someone had passed a duster over the surfaces as everything was clean and orderly. Despite the warm airlessness, the atmosphere was cosy and welcoming.

'I'll leave you to familiarise yourself in your own time,' Mr Kaye announced. 'I shall enjoy a stroll round the garden and a chat with Mr Warrender.'

Megan bestowed a grateful smile on

the thoughtful man.

'Thank you.'

She welcomed the solitude to acquaint herself with what she still found hard to believe was now her property. Walking down the narrow, stone-flagged passage, she explored the downstairs. Sunlight filled the rooms through leaded windows. After looking at a dining-room and a small study, she found a large living-room, featuring a massive, open fireplace. She imagined the heat and flickering firelight curling through the room in the winter months.

All the rooms had low, beamed ceilings, and the rough-textured walls were decorated in a wash of bright, pastel colours.

The kitchen, she discovered, was large and roomy, and painted daffodil yellow. Crossing the tiled floor, Megan raised the roller blind that shaded the window over the sink and gazed out at the garden. She could see Mr Kaye meandering along a twisting, gravel pathway, inspecting a well-stocked and colourful border.

Turning her back on the scene, Megan went upstairs. The first door opened on to a small bathroom decorated in cream and the palest peach. Next to it, and also looking over the driveway, was a plain and practical bedroom. The final door on the opposite side of the carpeted passage entered the main bedroom.

Stepping inside, Megan discovered that what had been two rooms had been knocked together as one, occupying the whole back of the cottage. The view over the garden and countryside to the sweep of the Downs was incredible. Slipping off a shoe, she sank her toes into the deep, soft white carpet. Like the rest of the furniture, the bed was pine, a huge four-poster draped in swirls of white silk and lace. The fabric on the bed and curtains that scooped the windows matched.

The whiteness continued in the decoration, but far from seeming stark, the room had an airy brightness that enchanted her. Owning the cottage had begun to appeal, Megan realised as she made her way back down the stairs. It was a foreign environment, and yet she felt drawn to this place in a way she could not explain, even to herself.

As Mr Kaye had not returned, Megan let herself out of the kitchen door and walked along the gravel path in the direction he had taken. The garden, with is hidden corners, was much larger than she had anticipated. Enjoying the feel of the sun on her skin, she ducked through a rose-covered archway and found herself in a wilder, more rambling part of the garden.

The air was heavy with intoxicating scents. As she wandered along the pathway, attracted by the distant murmur of masculine voices, she acknowledged that whoever Mr Warrender was he certainly knew a thing or two about plants and gardens. Megan rounded a corner and saw the two men sitting on a stone wall that surrounded a pond. She paused, absorbing her latest surprise. The man with Mr Kaye was not the kind of crusty, old gardener she had envisaged — far from it.

With hesitant steps, Megan moved forward, aware in some inner part of herself the exact moment she became the object of the stranger's attention. She swallowed, an instinctive, involuntary action as the man rose to his feet. Barely aware of Mr Kaye, her gaze locked on the younger man. His black hair glistened like polished ebony in the sunlight. Thick and straight, its disarray somehow seemed to characterise the man's whole persona — wild, abandoned, earthy. The impression was instantaneous, strong, fascinating, disturbing.

His face was appealing without being film-star perfect. His gaze met hers, studying her with a lazy intensity, his eyes thickly-lashed, their colour a deep grey.

'This is Mr Warrender, my dear,' Mr Kaye introduced, momentarily deflecting her attention.

'Miss Fitzgerald.'

Her name, spoke in a warm, smoky voice, drew her gaze smartly back to him.

'How do you do, Mr Warrender?'

'Luke, please.'

He wiped a dusty hand across the front of his green T-shirt before extending it towards her. Megan hesitated, unaccountably afraid to place her own hand in his. His touch was firm and lingered far longer than politeness dictated. Rattled, Megan withdrew her hand and stepped back a pace, evading his gaze.

'What did you think of the cottage?' Mr Kaye enquired, seemingly unaware of the charge of tension that flowed around him.

'It's beautiful. I love it.'

Luke shifted lazily before her, hooking his thumbs into the pockets of his work-worn jeans.

'Then you'll be coming to live here?'

'I haven't decided,' she responded, unable to deduce from his husky drawl whether he approved or disapproved of the idea.

'It's early days,' Mr Kaye intervened. 'I expect you may like to come back and spend some time here to get the feel of things.'

'Perhaps,' Megan conceded, warming to the idea.

'The cottage is yours to do with as you wish,' the solicitor confirmed, handing her the keys.

Megan held them in her hands — her keys, to her cottage. She looked up at Mr Kaye and smiled.

'Thank you.'

'I am sure Mr Warrender will be on hand to look after you,' Mr Kaye beamed, satisfied at the happy outcome.

Luke folded his bare arms, the tanned, hair-brushed flesh bunching with muscle, making her more conscious than ever of his strength, his masculine earthiness. Disconcerted at the prospect, Megan met the enigmatic grey gaze once more.

'I'll be here,' he agreed huskily. 'I'll see you again, Miss Fitzgerald.'

As Megan was ushered back towards the cottage by Mr Kaye, she wasn't sure if Luke's parting words had been a threat or a promise.

★ ★ ★

'Luke! Just the man!'

Trapped near the freezer in the village store, Luke smothered a sigh and turned to face the owner of the familiar, booming voice.

'Spill the beans,' Mabel Atkins demanded without preamble, her voice ringing with the authority she deemed her position as church organist and chairwoman of the Women's Institute afforded her. 'What is this girl like? Word has it you are the only one to have seen her.'

Word had spread already?

'For a couple of minutes, that's all,' Luke informed her, knowing it was useless to pretend not to know to whom the village busybody was referring.

'And?'

'She's OK, I suppose.'

Turning away, Luke studied the contents of the freezer. He had described Megan Fitzgerald as OK? So why hadn't he been able to get her out of his mind in the two days since she had visited the cottage? Angry with himself, he tossed a pizza and some frozen veg in his basket.

'Well?' Mabel boomed.

'Well what?'

'Is she young, pretty, what?'

'I didn't really notice,' he lied, trying to inch round Mabel and escape to the checkout.

With a surprisingly mischievous light in her keen blue eyes, Mabel fixed him with a knowing smile.

'I find it hard to believe a red-blooded man such as yourself failed to notice a young lady, Luke!'

The fact that Megan Fitzgerald had been impossible to ignore was not something he was about to discuss with anyone, least of all Mabel Atkins.

Framing a face that was at once delicate yet strong, and also quite heart-stoppingly beautiful, Megan's hair was the colour of a polished chestnut fresh from its husk. Snapping off his thoughts with a self-mocking grimace, Luke manoeuvred his way down the shop.

'One thing I can tell you,' he confided to the group huddled gossiping at the till, 'I was startled that Megan Fitzgerald looked so much like Sophie.'

Having paid for his purchases, Luke left the interested group pondering his words and walked home. He wondered what ramifications might follow the discharge of Sophie's will. She had wanted her niece to fill the emptiness of Honeysuckle Cottage. Having met her, Luke had the uncomfortable feeling that if she decided to stay, Megan Fitzgerald would not leave their lives untouched.

5

Although she had not owned a car since the battered orange banger of her university days, Megan was a competent and confident driver, and experienced no problems negotiating Sophie's Renault Clio through the congested London traffic.

Having driven the car back to Helen's flat after saying her goodbyes to Mr Kaye, she had spent a few days in the city seeing friends and tying up loose ends. Now, having stowed her personal belongings in the surprisingly roomy hatchback, she headed towards the motorway. Excitement filled her, masking whatever uncertainty lingered as she embarked on her adventure.

In the days since she had learned the full extent of her good fortune, she had been thinking about her future. The only decision she had reached was not to rush into anything.

Time at Honeysuckle Cottage, as Mr Kaye had suggested, would soon determine whether or not life in a country village was for her.

'You could always keep the cottage as a holiday retreat,' Helen had pointed out longingly as they talked late into the night. 'Just think of your poor London friends gasping for some country air.'

'I'm not doing anything in a hurry. I may hate it, or I may decide to stay and look for work in Brighton. I just don't know yet.'

'You could always work from home. You have the skills and you have always wanted to branch out. Why not start your own business?'

Helen's suggestion had taken root and it was an idea she was definitely considering with growing enthusiasm. Leaving the worst of the traffic behind her, Megan frowned as she thought back over the rest of their conversation the evening before.

'And what about him?' Helen had probed.

'Who?'

'The gardener, silly! Luke whatever-his-name-is!'

'I know nothing about him. I doubt I shall even see him. He was looking after Sophie's place for the solicitor, that is all.'

Megan acknowledged that her unwillingness to think or talk about Luke Warrender persisted. Why, she was still not sure, but despite her determination to the contrary, his image had refused to be banished from her mind.

When she finally reached her destination, she sat for a moment and looked at the cottage in the late afternoon light, feeling a glow of pleasure that it was hers. Bless the unknown Sophie for her generosity. She vowed to learn all she could about her benefactress while she was here.

After flinging open all the windows, letting the clear, scent-laden air wash the mustiness from the lonely rooms,

Megan carried her belongings inside and set about making herself at home. The cottage was even more charming than she remembered.

By evening, the cottage was beginning to feel aired and comfortable, with books on the shelves, magazines on the low table by the fireplace, and some flowers she had cut from the garden arranged in vases she had found in the kitchen cupboards.

The garden inevitably made her think of Luke. She wondered how often he came to maintain it and if he would still do so now she had taken possession of the cottage. Had he known Sophie, she wondered, or had he been engaged to maintain things by Mr Kaye? Frowning, Megan poured herself a glass of wine from the celebratory bottle Helen and Matt had given her. She carried it outside.

The warmth of the evening relaxed her. For a while she wandered the garden in the dimming light, savouring the stillness, suddenly disconcerted to find herself by the raised pond, the place she had first set eyes on Luke Warrender. When would she see him again, and why did the anticipation of it bring a flutter of uncertainty?

As she slid between the cool, crisp sheets of the unfamiliar bed a while later, a hint of a breeze toyed with the curtains at the windows, bringing with it the fragrance of jasmine and night-scented stock. Conscious of the unusual sounds of the countryside at night, Megan drifted off to sleep.

She woke to sunlight and birdsong. She pulled on a T-shirt and an old pair of jeans before crossing to the window, ready to face the challenges her new life here would present.

With a start of surprise she saw Luke already at work in the garden below. From her vantage point, she gazed at him unobserved, a knot of unwanted awareness clenching uncomfortably inside her. When he straightened and glanced up at her window, Megan jumped back behind the curtains. Had he sensed her watching him? She peeped out cautiously, seeing him run a hand across his brow before he resumed his work.

Perhaps she could just ignore that he was here or hope he would complete his work and leave without her having to talk to him. Megan hesitated, uncertain. Why was she so reluctant to see him again? What was it about Luke Warrender that had her in such a spin? Annoyed at her uncharacteristic timidity, she headed downstairs to the kitchen with purposeful steps.

'Good morning.'

The sound of Luke's voice had Megan swinging round from spooning coffee granules into the cafetière. Clutching the jar protectively against her chest, she observed him framed in the open back door. The material of his T-shirt hugged his body like a second skin.

Dark and brooding, he was just as disconcerting as she remembered.

' 'Morning,' she managed in reply.

'Is that coffee you're making?'

'Yes. Would you care for a cup?'

The ghost of a smile softened his mouth.

'I'd love one, thanks. Black, no sugar,' he added, stepping inside.

The room seemed to shrink with his presence in it. Megan busied herself with the coffee, anything to gain some breathing space. Aware of him washing his hands at the sink, she searched for the mugs.

'Second door on the left above you,' he offered, betraying his familiarity with the kitchen layout.

'Thank you.'

Megan opened the door and took down the mugs. She wasn't entirely comfortable that he seemed so relaxed and at home in the cottage which was so new to her.

'Please, sit down,' she invited, hoping he would seem less imposing with the table between them. He didn't!

She took a seat opposite him, pressing the plunger on the cafetière, before pouring the coffee and passing him a mug.

'Thanks.'

His gaze rested on her as she poured milk into her own drink and added a teaspoonful of sugar. She felt as if she was under assessment, as if Luke was testing her in some way, but she had no idea why, or if she passed. Tension seemed to crackle in the air between them, and she searched for something to say to break the silence.

'Will you stay on here?'

One dark eyebrow rose in questioning amusement.

'That depends what you want me to do for you, Miss Fitzgerald.'

'My name is Megan, please, and I meant that I know very little about gardening. You've been doing such a good job here, I had hoped we could continue with the arrangement,' she clarified with a spark of irritation and embarrassment.

Amusement remained in the depths of his eyes.

'I'll be pleased to carry on in the garden, Megan.'

His smoky voice made her name sound like a caress. Disconcerted, Megan tucked a stray strand of hair behind one ear. Taking a reviving sip of coffee, she strove to change the subject.

'Did you know Sophie well?'

His gaze slid from hers, but not before his expression closed and all traces of amusement were erased from his eyes.

'Yes. Yes, I did.'

Megan watched him for a moment, intrigued. His answer had raised a whole new batch of questions. Just how well had he known Sophie? Had it been a working relationship, or something more?

'I wish I had known of her sooner and had been able to meet her,' she told him, needing to know more about the unexpected relative who had been so thoughtful and generous. 'What was she like?'

'Warm, funny, caring, inquisitive,

intelligent, loyal . . . '

Megan's speculation increased at the edge of loss in his voice. Clearly speaking of Sophie was difficult for him, and clearly she had been important to him, someone he respected and cared about. Megan had so many questions she wanted to ask, but she hesitated, unsure how far she could push Luke on the subject. He took the decision out of her hands by draining the last of his drink and rising to his feet.

'I'd better go. I have a job to get to,' he explained, washing and drying his mug.

Megan smothered an unexpected rush of disappointment.

'Thank you for stopping by,' she murmured politely, leaving her chair to see him out.

'Thanks for the coffee.'

A sudden smile eased across his serious expression and he surprised her by taking her hand in his, the work-roughened fingers caressing briefly, enticingly, before he released her.

'I know Sophie would be pleased you are here. Finding you meant a lot to her. I hope you'll be very happy in the cottage.'

Touched, Megan returned his smile.

'Thank you.'

'Sophie was well-liked in the village. I'm sure you'll find her friends will make you welcome.'

'I'll look forward to meeting them.'

He hesitated as he turned for the door.

'You can certainly expect a visit from Mabel Atkins before long! She likes to see herself as the matriarch of the village and keeps her finger on the pulse of everything that goes on. She chatters, but she's harmless enough.'

'I appreciate being forewarned!'

He gave a brief nod, his intense gaze holding hers.

'I'll be around. If you need anything, just ask.'

'Thanks.'

As he walked outside and along the

path to the drive, Megan left the kitchen, the stone-flagged passage cool beneath her bare feet. She stood at the window in the hall watching as Luke stowed his tools in the back of the van. Then, slipping on a pair of sunglasses, he strode to the driver's door with a lazy, loose-limbed gait.

After the van had left, disappearing behind the hedgerow, Megan gave a little shiver, running her hands along her arms, finding that despite the heat of the day, she had goosebumps. There was something about Luke that made her wary. Both he and the cottage seemed to have cast a spell over her.

Sophie's legacy had set her on an uncharted journey. Now she had two choices. She could run back to all that was safe and familiar, or she could stay and embrace the unknown.

Megan allowed a small smile, her decision already made. There was really no choice at all.

6

Megan found the days passed swiftly as she learned her way around and explored the village. She went to the shop each day for fresh produce and a newspaper, used now to the curiosity her presence aroused and the speculation about her plans.

The gentle invasion of her privacy had unsettled her at first, but everyone had been friendly, softening the unaccustomed interest in her affairs. As Luke had predicted, Mabel Atkins had been her first caller. Megan had felt politeness dictated that she ask her in and serve her tea, and there had followed an hour of none-too-subtle questioning and probing about herself and her background.

Thinking of Luke's warning, Megan had smothered a smile and borne the intrusion with good grace. The stout, busy woman had also given her what seemed to be a potted history on just about everyone in the village. Mabel was certainly a mine of information!

'You definitely have a strong look of Sophie about you,' she had pronounced before she left. 'Such a nice woman, something of a celebrity in these parts. Did you know she wrote?'

'Mr Kaye, the solicitor, did tell me. I've found copies of her work here which I'm sure I shall enjoy,' Megan replied politely.

Mabel nodded in approval.

'Good, good. Now, I must be off, I'm afraid.'

She checked her watch and heaved herself from the armchair. Quite glad the interview had come to an end, Megan smiled warmly.

'Thank you for coming.'

'Always keen to welcome new people, and be sure to let me know if there is anything I can do,' Mabel added, hooking a bulging handbag over her arm.

'I will.'

'Are you a gardener, Megan?'

'No, I'm afraid not,' she admitted, gently guiding her chatty guest towards the door.

'Well, I expect Luke will continue to take care of the garden for you.'

She hesitated on the front step, her voice lowering as she imparted another confidence.

'Of course, we know nothing much about his background, you understand, but he's liked here and certainly has a good business going with the landscaping. Sophie championed him.'

This last was clearly meant to be a final seal of approval, Megan decided, watching as Mabel waved and waddled off down the drive. Closing the door, Megan leaned against it for a moment, feeling as if she had been run over!

Luke had taken to stopping by first thing to work on the garden before setting off for whatever other business he took care of during the day. Despite her continued wariness of him, it became a routine for him to stop in for a coffee with her in the kitchen.

'Mabel called yesterday afternoon,' she told him the next morning.

Flint grey eyes lightened with amusement.

'Ah! I didn't think it would be long.'

'Is she always so . . . well, such . . . '

'Such a nosy gossip?' he finished for her as she stumbled for the words. 'Yes!'

Megan laughed.

'She seems to know everything about everybody.'

'She certainly tries.'

Megan let the subject drop. Something in Luke's tone suggested he disliked probing and gossip. For all her talk, Mabel had known little about him, Megan recalled, a small frown creasing her brow.

Later, she walked to the post office, her mind questioning once more what it was about Luke that was so prickly. One moment he was an intelligent, even humorous companion, but if you unwittingly crossed some unexplained

69

and unseen boundary, he closed up like a clam, unapproachable, guarded, withdrawn.

'Hi, Megan!'

Jolted from her thoughts by the sound of the friendly voice, Megan turned to smile at Catherine, a leggy blonde a few years older than herself, whom Megan had met on her first full day in the village.

'Hello, Catherine, how is the family?' Megan enquired, knowing one of her small children had been poorly.

'All fit and flourishing now, thanks. Are you settling in all right?'

'Fine. I'm amazed how little I miss London.'

She had learned much general local information from Catherine, not least that she and Sophie had been friends.

'Everyone was friends with Sophie,' Catherine had said with a smile. 'You couldn't help but like her. She was a very kind person and always had time for people and their problems.'

Now, as they neared the village shop,

Catherine halted and put a hand on Megan's arm.

'I'm meeting a few friends for a drink at the pub tonight. My husband, Jeff, is looking after the kids. Why don't you join us?'

'Are you sure I won't be in the way?'

'Goodness, don't be daft! The more the merrier. It will be an excellent opportunity for you to meet people. Do say you'll come.'

Pleased by her new friend's warm invitation, Megan accepted happily, smiling at the genuine delight on Catherine's face.

Her shopping completed and arrangements made with Catherine for meeting later, Megan made her way home. Scooping up a wad of envelopes from the doormat, she carried them through to the kitchen, putting her shopping away before turning her attention to her post.

Apart from a circular and a couple of letters from friends, including Helen, there was a lilac-hued envelope addressed to her in an unfamiliar, flowery hand. Puzzled, Megan tore open the envelope and found inside a couple of sheets of faintly-perfumed paper.

Dear Megan, she read,
If you are reading this, then Mr Kaye has found you, you have accepted the legacy, and what I have longed for has happened. I wish that we had met, that my time had not run out, but it was not to be. I can only hope that my instincts were right, and that the feelings I had about you being a kindred spirit prove to be true.

Will you uncover the secrets of the cottage, Megan, and embrace the full extent of my legacy to you? I hope you will be as happy there as I have been. Now follow the clues! First you must ask Cupid for the key!
With love,
Sophie.

Megan frowned as she read the letter again, excitement bubbling inside her.

The key to what? Where would she find Cupid? Why had Sophie set her this intriguing treasure hunt?

Her curiosity growing, Megan began a detailed search, delving into every nook and cranny, checking cupboards, pictures, everything she could think of in her quest for the Roman god of love. By late afternoon, she wanted to stamp in angry frustration. It had to be somewhere. She just had to think it out.

'Use your brain, Megan,' she muttered to herself, wondering who had posted Sophie's letter to her.

Had it been Mr Kaye discharging more of his duties? Had it been Luke, still an unknown quantity? Or was it someone else, someone as yet undiscovered, who was directing this scene Sophie had created? To whom was she supposed to turn? Where was Sophie trying to lead her?

She had almost abandoned the search for the day when she had a sudden brainwave. What about the pond? That statue, she thought, making her way down the garden. Wasn't that Cupid?

'Yes!' she exclaimed, filled with a burst of triumph as she reached the statue.

And what was that? Hanging by a piece of purple ribbon from the tip of the figure's arrow was an envelope! It hadn't been there before. Who had left it? Luke? Someone else?

Reaching out precariously over the water, Megan grasped the envelope, surprised at its weight. Inside she found another note along with an old key.

Well done, Megan! So far so good! Now find the lock the key fits. Happy hunting, Sophie.

She turned the large, heavy key over in her hand. What would it open? And what would she find when she solved the next clue?

Dismayed by the time, not wanting to

be late meeting Catherine and her friends, Megan knew that following the next stage of Sophie's trail would have to wait until later.

With a measure of regret at what she was leaving behind, Megan changed and hurried down the lane to the village pub. The White Horse was not the most attractive of buildings, but the profusion of tubs and hanging baskets outside, overflowing with a riot of colour, softened the sombre façade.

As she stepped inside, her gaze scanning the crowded interior for Catherine, Megan noted the oak beams and horse brasses, and the open fireplaces that would be welcoming to gather round on cold winter days.

'Megan!'

She turned at the sound of her name, seeing her friend waving from a doorway across the room. Easing her way across, Megan joined her.

'Hi.'

'I'm so glad you came,' Catherine

said with a big grin. 'Come on, we're out here on the patio. It's such a lovely evening. Let me introduce you to everyone, then I'll get the drinks. What are you having?'

Within moments, Megan found herself at ease in the group. They were all women in their late twenties or early thirties, a mixed, interesting crowd, and Megan was soon glad she had come. A drink in her hand, a smile on her face, she was drawn in to the lively conversation, sharing the laughter, included in the village gossip, the discussion of the latest books, the friendly arguments about politics.

'Oh, crikey!' one of the women exclaimed, breaking into the chatter.

'What is it?' Catherine asked.

'Dominic.'

Catherine's eyes widened and she swung round on the bench to stare towards the entrance. A small frown puckering her brows, she turned to Megan.

'You haven't met Dominic yet, have you?'

'No, should I have?'

'Well, I think I ought to tell you that — '

Catherine grimaced, her words abandoned as a figure arrived beside them. Megan looked up at the newcomer, surprised when her heart gave a flutter. Dressed in a smart suit, Dominic was tall, athletic-looking, with dark blond hair, hazel eyes and a devastating smile.

'I have been longing to meet you, Megan,' he greeted her when they had been introduced. 'I was so hoping you would come to the village.'

Taken aback, Megan smiled.

'Were you?'

'Absolutely.'

The roguish smile flashed again as he pulled up a chair beside her. As the conversation resumed around them, he gave her his undivided attention, intriguing her, charming her with his cultured manner, his wit and ready intelligence. So engrossed was she that she barely realised when the others began to drift away. It was only when Catherine touched her arm and wished her good-night, a flicker of unease in her eyes, that Megan realised how much time had sped by. She had not even noticed that dusk had given way to a moonlit night.

'I didn't realise it was so late,' she murmured in confusion.

Dominic smiled.

'At least I haven't bored you.'

'Of course not.'

Megan took a last look after her friend's retreating figure. Had she imagined the disappointment or disapproval in her eyes?

'I hope Catherine's not upset about something.'

'Probably a bit envious that I've been monopolising you.'

Megan couldn't imagine Catherine was that insecure.

'Please,' Dominic began, claiming her attention, 'let me walk you home.'

'That's not necessary.'

He smiled again, taking her hand as they rose to their feet.

'I know, but indulge me. I'll enjoy spending more time with you.'

Lulled by the ambience of the evening, Megan accepted, forgetting every word of her resolve not to have anything more to do with men after the rawness of her experience with Stuart. Something about Dominic was very attractive and persuasive!

'So,' Dominic said as they strolled along under the starry sky, 'you never actually knew Sophie.'

'Sadly not until the solicitor contacted me but by then it was too late.'

'She was very determined to find you. We were close, Sophie and I,' he confided. 'Very close. I know how much she had hoped to meet you.'

An owl hooted in the wood nearby, startling her, and Dominic stepped closer, slipping a reassuring arm around her shoulders.

Was it just coincidence that he had turned up now, Megan wondered, just when the letter had arrived and the clue had been left on the statue? Was Dominic perhaps the missing piece in the puzzle?

'I hope you'll stay here, Megan, and I hope that we see more of each other.'

Dominic smiled, as they reached the cottage. He released her as Megan searched for her key.

'That would be nice,' she replied.

'Will you come out to dinner with me one evening? How about Friday?'

'I'd like that, thank you,' she agreed, turning to face him with a smile.

His fingers feathered softly over her cheek before he bent his head, replacing the touch with the brush of his lips.

'I'll pick you up on Friday about seven,' he murmured, promise in the tone of his voice. 'And don't worry what anyone else thinks.'

'What do you mean?' she queried, her pleasure in the evening dampened by the veiled warning.

'Only that there may be those who wish you had not come here and claimed the cottage.'

'Everyone has been very friendly and welcoming.'

'I'm sure they have, it's just . . . '

Stepping back to view him under the light of the porch, Megan's frown deepened.

'Just what?'

'Well, the talk is that Luke Warrender, for one, had hopes of inheriting, but I don't know. Some people may not be all they seem, that's all.'

Seeing her concerned expression, he shook his head.

'I shouldn't have mentioned it. It was clumsy of me. You can rest assured that those of us who cared for Sophie will care for you.'

A sudden chill swept through her. She watched as Dominic walked away into the night, suddenly no longer sure about her place here, or the people she had met. For all Dominic's hasty reassurances, how could she know who was her friend? Whom could she trust? After a troubled night, Megan woke late the next morning to the ringing of the telephone.

'Hello?' she answered sleepily.

'Hope I'm not interrupting anything!' Helen's voice teased with her usual irrepressible spirit, bright, breezy and full of mischief.

Megan grinned.

'Of course not! I just had a lie in.'

'All right for some!'

'What about you? Why aren't you at work?'

'I have the morning off for a dentist appointment at eleven so thought I'd ring for a chat before I left.'

Rolling over, Megan made herself comfortable.

'I'm very glad you did. It's a tonic to hear your voice.'

'So, how are things?'

Relieved to be able to talk, Megan gave her friend an edited version of events since they had last spoken.

'A treasure hunt? How exciting!'

'I know, but I've yet to find the lock the key fits. I'm going to have a search today. I can't wait to find out what Sophie has hidden, and why.'

'It's all very mysterious,' Helen agreed. 'And what about this other man, Dominic, you said? What's he like?'

'Very good-looking, charming, and apparently was a close friend of Sophie's.'

'And he's already asking you out to dinner? That was fast work!'

Helen's teasing failed to banish the hint of uneasiness that still lingered in Megan's mind after Dominic's parting words the night before. She decided not to worry her friend about her concerns over the secrets and puzzles still to be resolved.

'I'll let you know how it goes,' she promised.

'How is Matt?'

'Fantastic!'

Megan laughed at Helen's delicious sigh.

'And?'

'He's moving in.'

'And you say my being invited for dinner was quick work?' she teased back, hearing Helen's laughter. 'Tell you what, why don't you both come down and spend the weekend with me?'

Her friend's delight was obvious.

'We'd love to! Oh, Megan, I can't wait to see you, and I'm longing to see the cottage and the village, and the two handsome men you have dangling!'

'I do not!'

'If you say so! Gosh, is that the time? I'll have to fly. Happy hunting!'

Cheered by her friend's call, Megan had a hurried, late breakfast, wondering if Luke had been that morning, glad she had missed him if he had. She didn't feel like coping with him, or anyone, until she had answers for some of the questions that were plaguing her. Taking Sophie's note and the key, she set her other concerns aside and concentrated on her search.

Beginning downstairs, Megan went methodically through each room, but all the doors opened, and the only piece of furniture she found with a lock and no key was the bureau in the study, and the old key in her hand was far too big for that. There was nothing in the garage, either, so she went upstairs, somewhat deflated at her failure to solve the latest stage of Sophie's riddle. She couldn't find anything in the bedrooms that the key would fit, the bathroom likewise.

After a fruitless search, Megan gave up her quest, unable to spend the whole day on the task. She would return to the hunt tomorrow, she promised herself, when she felt refreshed. Hopefully inspiration would strike then.

The next morning proved just as frustrating, however. She slumped down on the bed, disappointed at her lack of success. Dispirited, she lay on her stomach, her fingers toying with the carved rail at the foot of the bed. Where else could she look? Was this just a wild-goose chase? Idly, her fingers moved to straighten the embroidered cloth that rested on the top of the blanket chest at the foot of the bed.

The chest!

Heart pounding, Megan scrambled off the bed. Had she found her answer?

7

Megan tossed the cloth aside. It was an ancient, oak chest with the initials **JMU** carved on the top.

Kneeling on the carpeted floor, Megan tried the key, holding her breath as it met some initial resistance, but it did fit! The hinges creaked as she opened the lid. She wasn't sure what she expected to find inside, what Sophie had hidden away for her eyes only. There were a number of wrapped parcels, on top of which was a sheet of paper, the flamboyant writing now familiar to her.

You're doing well, Megan. I entrust the enclosed to you. Sophie.

Intrigued, Megan set the note aside. Sitting back on her heels, she lifted out the first parcel, carefully removing the brown wrapping. Inside she found an old photograph album. Sophie had carefully catalogued each print, Megan discovered, realising she held her family history in her hands. These were the faces of grandparents and relatives she had never known existed until Mr Kaye had broken the shocking news of her inheritance.

Unaware of time, Megan went through each item she uncovered — family photographs, letters, documents, all manner of things that brought the generations alive. Sophie had done more than leave her a house and a sum of money. She had given her the family, the sense of belonging she had never known before.

Overcome with the emotions of her discoveries, Megan admitted it would take time to piece together all the history and family secrets the letters and documents contained. It was a task she would enjoy in the days to come, learning all about her heritage, uncovering why her grandfather, Sophie's father, John Malcolm Unsworth, had been banished, and why the split in the family had been so irrevocable.

She was about to close the lid, believing she had examined the last of the carefully-stored packages, when she noticed a small envelope on the paper lining the bottom of the chest. Taking it out, she tore open the envelope and found another note from Sophie.

Still with me, Megan? I hope these things will fill any gaps you may have, and also help to explain why I so wanted you to come here, why I chose you to be my heir. And now for the next clue! Yes, there's more! Find the secret drawer, Megan. If you can, you'll hopefully uncover the last of my gifts to you.

As ever, Sophie.

Megan put all the albums and packages back in the chest for safe-keeping and locked the chest. She would go through them thoroughly soon. Slipping the key into her pocket, puzzled at what else Sophie could have left for her, she went back downstairs, surprised to find that the afternoon was almost over. Her tummy rumbled in complaint at her missed lunch, but she ignored it, anxious to find the secret drawer.

Surely the bureau was the logical place to start. But try as she might, running her fingers over it and pressing various places, Megan could find no clues to the location of Sophie's hiding place. Frustrated, she glanced at her watch, painfully aware of the passing of time. She would need to abandon her search and get changed if she was to be ready for Dominic's arrival.

She had just finished drying her hair after a quick shower when the doorbell rang. Surely he couldn't be this early. She cursed, tightening her robe around her and rushing barefoot down the stairs. She flung open the front door and took a step back in surprise when she saw Luke waiting in the porch.

'Oh!' she exclaimed.

'Sorry,' he said, appearing awkward and uncertain, his gaze flicking over her and turning away again. 'I was just wondering if you'd like to come down to the pub for a drink.'

Taken aback by the unexpected invitation, and its timing, Megan grimaced.

'It's really kind of you, Luke, but I'm going out this evening. I was just getting ready.'

'You're seeing someone?'

Luke's intense gaze bored into her eyes as he delivered his statement. Feeling uncomfortable, still wary of him and unsure, Megan shrugged.

'Sort of,' she responded. 'Tonight, anyway.'

'Of course. It was silly of me not to have thought. Sorry I bothered you.'

'No, it's OK,' she began, but Luke was already walking away, his shoulders tense, his back erect.

Megan muttered as she shut the front door and dashed back upstairs to dress.

Why now, of all times, had Luke delivered his invitation? And why had he been unusually reticent and unsure of himself? It was quite out of character for the controlled, self-possessed man she had witnessed over the last few days.

Before she could assess her thoughts, the doorbell sounded again. Slipping her feet into her shoes, she picked up her bag and went back downstairs once more. Dominic was all smiles and charm, offering her a big bunch of flowers and a box of chocolates.

'Thank you,' she murmured. 'I'll just put the flowers in some water.'

She wasn't entirely comfortable that Dominic invited himself in and followed close behind her into the kitchen. She wondered if he was always so ardent and effusive, or if he had singled her out for special attention because of Sophie. Despite his open friendliness and obvious keenness, a twinge of doubt remained.

'The place hasn't lost any of its

warm, homely feel,' he commented in approval, glancing round the ground floor of the cottage.

'I'm glad.'

Megan hesitated, unsure if she should offer him a drink or something before they left, but fortunately, he smiled and suggested it was time they left.

'I've booked a table at an excellent Italian restaurant,' he told her as they walked outside to his flashy sports car. 'I hope that's all right.'

'Lovely.'

The journey passed quickly. Dominic chatted about his job as sales director at a local firm selling prestigious cars. No doubt his easy charm and patter were a godsend in his work, Megan allowed with a smile. He could probably sell freezers in the Arctic!

By the time they were seated and studying the menu, Dominic had managed to discover far more about her, from her days at university to her recent redundancy.

'The news of the legacy must have been doubly welcome,' he observed, watching as she sipped her wine.

'Yes, in way, of course,' Megan agreed, cautious not to give away too much. 'At least it gives me some breathing space while I decide what to do.'

'And have you any plans?'

'I'm not sure yet. I have been toying with the idea of doing web design from home, but, well, we'll see.'

'Go for it, if that's what you want,' Dominic encouraged with enthusiastic support. 'You are planning on staying in the village then?'

Megan took another sip of her drink.

'For the time being,' she allowed, wondering why she was so reluctant to divulge too much to this man.

He changed the subject, speaking of his family, his successful parents and his two older sisters, one a solicitor, one a doctor. Megan was interested, but shared little information about her own family situation. She also made no mention of Sophie's notes and the hidden items she was uncovering at the cottage.

The meal was delicious and she soon found herself relaxing in the pleasing atmosphere and with Dominic's charming company. Throughout the meal, she remained the focus of his attention, beguiled by his intelligence and good humour.

'Sophie was a wonderful person,' he confided. 'We all cared for her so much. She would be so delighted you are here.'

'I wish I could have met her.'

'It was what she wanted most, too.'

Resting her arms on the table, lingering over coffee, Megan smiled.

'Tell me more about her. How did you meet?'

'At a mutual friend's party,' Dominic told her with a small laugh as if the memory pleased him. 'She was stunning, sharp, funny. I was quite captivated the moment I saw her.'

'It must have been very hard when she became ill.'

A veil shielded the expression in his eyes.

'Of course. It was absolutely tragic. I really don't like to talk about it, even now. Maybe it sounds odd, but I prefer to remember her as she was at her most alive.'

'No, I understand,' Megan conceded, a small frown creasing her brow.

'She was a very generous person, anyway, always taking in waifs and strays, like Luke, I suppose.'

Megan stiffened as he turned once again to the subject of Luke, implying she should be wary of him. Just what did Dominic have against Luke? Why was he so intent on warning her off?

'I gather you and Luke Warrender are not friends,' she commented.

'Hardly!'

Dominic pulled a face and shrugged his shoulder.

'Not that I know him that well, to be honest.'

'Then why the antagonism?'

'He was one of Sophie's causes. There's something very unsavoury about his past and I was always wary of the way he hung around her and the cottage so much.'

'Perhaps Sophie was happy with the work he was doing in the garden,' Megan pointed out, irritated that a fresh wave of doubt should threaten to spoil her evening.

'Perhaps,' Dominic agreed, uncertainty heavy in his voice.

She changed the subject, but her doubts remained. Was there something not quite right about Luke? Mr Kaye appeared to trust him, but why was Dominic so ready to speak against Luke? Just how close a relationship had either man had with Sophie?

Instead of finding any kind of answers or reassurance, Megan found herself more confused than ever. How could she find out the truth? How could she know who her allies really were in the village? Only Sophie knew the answers, and the only way to find out what she needed to know was to locate the secret drawer and find the missing pieces to the puzzle.

8

Saturday morning dawned bright and sunny, the sky a clear blue with only a couple of puffy white clouds trailing high in the atmosphere. Yawning, Megan made herself some coffee, carrying it outside to enjoy the solitude, thankful that there was no sign of Luke.

She frowned as she thought back to the events of the previous night. It was a shame that Dominic had spoiled things, sowing further doubts and leaving her more confused and unsettled than before. There was no doubt that he was a good-looking, charming companion, and she was attracted to him, but whether it was her memories of her time with Stuart that held her back or the uncertainties of her new situation, Megan was unsure.

The evening had not ended well, she

admitted, taking a reviving drink of her coffee. When Dominic had driven her home, they had stood under the trellis by the front door.

'I've enjoyed being with you, Megan. I'd like to see you again,' he had told her. 'Are you free any time over the weekend?'

'I have friends coming to stay,' she replied, somewhat relieved to have a genuine excuse.

Dominic was clearly disappointed.

'Next week then?'

'Perhaps.'

Seemingly reluctant to leave, he cupped her face in his hands and kissed her. It was enjoyable, and Megan felt herself responding. Yet, what was wrong, she wondered. He was skilled, practiced, but it seemed just as if it were an act, not something he had done with any real feeling.

'I'm very attracted to you,' he whispered.

Megan stepped back a pace. Why was he working so hard to impress her?

'I really enjoyed dinner,' she thanked him, bringing things to a halt. 'Goodnight, Dominic.'

The frown on his handsome face displayed his disappointment that she hadn't invited him in. Once more his attitude roused her suspicions. What was his hurry?

The sound of a vehicle pulling up outside the cottage roused her from her reverie. She popped through from the garden to the drive, wondering if Helen and Matt could possibly have arrived already. However, it was the postman's van that idled by the gate. Smiling, she went to collect her mail.

'Settling in all right?' he asked with a smile.

'Fine, thank you. Everyone has been so nice.'

'It's certainly a great place to live. Very different from what you are used to in the city, I imagine.'

'But no less enjoyable for that.'

Clearly of a mind to talk more, but anxious to finish his round, the postman sighed and put his van back in gear.

'Cheerio, Miss Fitzgerald.'

★ ★ ★

The rhythmic sound off his horse's hooves on the hard ground was rivalled only by birdsong and the faintest breeze whispering in the trees. It was a beautiful morning for a ride, but Luke found his mind too occupied to enjoy the pleasures of the day.

He was still cursing himself for being all manner of a fool. How could he have turned up at Megan's last night to ask her out for a drink? It was stupid of him to imagine she wouldn't be involved with someone. After all, he knew nothing at all about her life before she had arrived at the cottage, little more than a week ago.

He had always found it hard to talk to people, although Sophie had been an exception. In Megan, surprisingly, he was beginning to see many of the qualities of his old friend. Megan was younger, yes, her own person, but she was just as bright and alive as Sophie had been.

As Bob's post van came around a bend in the road, Luke slowed his horse's pace and moved aside.

'Lovely day,' Bob greeted him with a cheery wave as he inched past.

Luke nodded, controlling Morning Mist as she tossed her head and jigged impatiently.

'Easy girl,' he murmured, causing one of her ears to flick back in response to his voice.

The engine note of the van died as Bob continued on his round, and Luke ran a work-roughened hand along the thoroughbred's silken neck, feeling the warmth and quiver of muscle under the smooth coat.

'Let's get on, Misty.'

She jig-jogged sideways down the lane, full of spirit. As he approached Honeysuckle Cottage, he saw Megan at the gate flicking through a bundle of letters obviously just left by Bob. The sunlight gleamed on her hair, making it glow like burnished russet. Luke cursed again. Whatever had made him come down this way?

About to turn back to the house, Megan heard the horse's hooves in the lane and leaned on the gate to see who came by. Her eyes widened in surprise as she recognised Luke astride a frisky, dark grey horse.

The days since she had been here had done nothing to lessen his impact on her and she felt the familiar charge of alarm and awareness as he approached. She met the full force of his intent, flinty gaze.

'Megan,' he greeted, reining in his mount and pausing beside the gate.

'Hello, Luke.'

She had always found him unsettling, but now that Dominic had sown his horrible seeds of doubt, her unease increased. What did she know of him? He seemed to have free run of the cottage and garden, apparently with Mr

Kaye's approval, but was he to be trusted? What of Dominic's allusion to his unsavoury past?

'Everything all right?' he asked.

Startled by Luke's words, wondering if he sensed her disquiet, Megan nodded.

'I'm fine.'

'Did you have a good evening?'

'Very nice, thank you. I'm sorry, you know, about the pub.'

'That's OK. I just thought I could have introduced you to a few people.'

So he had just been polite?

'Of course.'

She smiled brightly, dispelling any unnecessary and misplaced disappointment.

The horse side-stepped impatiently, but quietened under the touch of Luke's hand.

'What's its name?' she asked.

'Morning Mist. Misty for short. She was Sophie's pride and joy,' he added, his expression sombre.

'Oh! I didn't realise.'

Megan took in this latest information. Even in her ignorance of things equestrian she could see the skill and ease with which Luke controlled the spirited animal, the rapport he seemed to have with it. This was one more piece to add to an already hazy jigsaw puzzle.

'Do you ride?' he queried, a small smile playing at the corner of his mouth.

'No. I always agreed with whoever it was who said horses were dangerous at both ends and uncomfortable in the middle.'

As Luke laughed, she realised it was the first time she had heard him do so. It was as if it was something he did not do very often, but it was infectious and brought a smile to her own face.

'Perhaps you should give it a try some time and find out for yourself.'

'I don't think so,' she declined with a nervous shake of her head at the thought.

His gaze slid from hers and swept over the wooded countryside.

'Well, I'd best let you get on.'

'I have some friends coming for the weekend,' she offered.

Luke turned back to face her, Misty moving impatiently beneath him.

'There's a village barbecue at the pub tonight. Bring your friends along. They'll be more than welcome.'

'Maybe I will,' Megan replied. 'Thanks.'

Touching the fingers of one hand to the rim of his hat in salute, Luke eased the lively horse away from the gate.

'Be seeing you, Megan.'

She watched as he rode away, still unsure what to make of him. Was she right to be wary? After all, why take Dominic's word? How did she know he was telling the truth about Luke? She knew so little about either of them.

Dominic claimed he had been close to Sophie and talked of her openly. Luke, on the other hand, guarded his secrets and his feelings closely, giving little away. It was a riddle, one to which she was determined to find answers.

9

'You're here!' Megan's excited exclamation had Helen laughing as she bounded from the car and hugged her friend.

'We are!' Helen grinned. 'It's brilliant to see you. I know it's only been about two weeks, but it seems an age since you left London.'

'Tell me about it!'

Megan stepped back and was enfolded in an affectionate bear hug by Matt.

'Hi!' he greeted, looking as handsome as ever.

'Hi, yourself! Thanks for coming, both of you.'

Megan helped take a bag from the boot.

'Let me show you upstairs so you can settle in, then we can talk.'

It was wonderful to see her best

friend again. A while later, they made iced drinks in the kitchen, and Megan looked Helen over.

'I have to say love agrees with you,' she said with a grin. 'You are positively glowing!'

A warm, happy blush pinkened Helen's cheeks.

'Matt is so fantastic. I'm really, really happy, Megan. I've never felt like this before.'

'I couldn't be more pleased for you,' she responded honestly, delighted to see her friend so content.

'This place is great,' Matt enthused as he joined them and they took their drinks out to the garden.

'Fab,' Helen agreed with equal fervour. 'It's lovely, Megan. So peaceful. I was really unsure if you could become a country bumpkin, but I think anyone could be happy here. There's an aura about it almost. I felt it as soon as we came in.'

After a salad lunch, they left Matt relaxing on a garden lounger, listening to a cricket match on the radio while Megan took Helen upstairs to show her the letters and photographs Sophie had stored in the chest.

'I wonder why she went to so much trouble to hide things and do the treasure hunt for you.'

'Me, too,' Megan agreed.

Helen pored over the photograph albums, enthralled.

'The family resemblance is extraordinary.'

'I know. It feels really odd.'

'Nice odd, or creepy odd?'

Megan grinned.

'Nice odd.'

Grinning back, Helen looked through some of the papers.

'They seem a very unforgiving lot, don't they? Your grandfather was always destined to remain the black sheep, and when he remarried, it was as if they disowned him entirely.'

'They did.'

'I suppose things were different back then.'

Megan nodded.

'That's what Mr Kaye said, but even so, I wonder what my mother really thought about it.'

'Did she never speak of him?'

'No, not of any of the family. But he was her father. Did she know what happened and if so, why did she keep it all so secret? And did she know about Sophie?'

'What I want to know,' Helen continued after a moment's pause, 'is how your grandfather found out about you.'

Megan frowned, sitting back on her heels on the carpeted floor.

'How do you mean?'

'Well, Sophie is older than you, so he was obviously cast out a long time before you came along. Someone must have told him,' Helen clarified, flicking through one of the photograph albums and passing it across. 'Here, didn't you see this page of you?'

'Where?'

Stunned, Megan took the album,

amazed she had missed what indeed proved to be three photos of herself, one as a baby, one when she was about four years old, and one taken a few years later.

'I wonder where he got them.'

'That's what I mean. It's the great unknown,' Helen continued. 'Clearly Sophie must have found all this stuff at some point and decided she wanted to locate you.'

Her grandfather must have kept this hidden from his new family, Megan realised, wondering when he had died, and when Sophie had discovered all the family history.

'It must have been quite recently from what Mr Kaye told me. It's just so sad to think that Sophie had become so ill before the quest was completed. I'd love to have known her.'

Helen nodded in sombre agreement as they closed the album.

'She looks and sounds a really lovely person.'

A moment of quiet reflection settled

over them. Megan knew that whatever the outcome of her puzzle, she was glad she had come here, glad she had discovered more about Sophie and her family.

'I still have the final, at least I think it's the final clue to unravel,' she commented as they made their way back downstairs. 'There's a secret drawer, in the bureau, I imagine, but I've not found it yet.'

That evening, they headed for The White Horse for the barbecue. Megan felt unaccountably nervous at seeing Luke, anxious, too, in case Dominic turned up. What would Helen make of the two men? She had given her friend brief details about her concerns, unsure whom she trusted and what rôle each had played in Sophie's life, but it sounded melodramatic when put into words.

Helen, however, had not teased her. Instead, she seemed interested and thoughtful.

'You mean you don't know what

either of their motives are in befriend-ing you?'

'Well, sort of, I suppose. I wouldn't say that Luke had set out to befriend me, exactly. He was just a sort of fixture from the first moment, but, yes, I suppose I do have the feeling that Dominic has sought me out.'

'Perhaps he just fancies you! Anyway, what you need to ask is if either of them has something to gain.'

Megan frowned.

'How so?'

'I don't know the terms of the will, but what would have happened if you had not inherited? Has someone lost out because Sophie left the cottage to you?'

Helen's words had nagged at her during the afternoon as it was an avenue she hadn't previously consid-ered, but it did make sense. The problem was she was no nearer solving the riddle of which man, if either, she could trust.

Her doubts were cast aside for the

moment as they were welcomed into the throngs of villagers spilling out of the pub into the gardens at the rear. Megan introduced Helen and Matt to several of the people she knew, then all three found themselves included in the group with Catherine, her husband, Jeff, and their children.

Megan felt rather than saw Luke. She glanced round, her gaze meeting his, as he stepped through the crowds to join them.

'I'm glad you came, Megan.'

'Thanks for telling me about it.'

A faint flush warmed her face as she turned to introduce him and saw the admiration and teasing speculation in Helen's gaze. Ignoring it, Megan steadied her voice.

'Luke, this is my best friend, Helen, and her partner, Matt.'

The introductions completed, Luke and Matt retreated to the bar to replenish the drinks.

'You didn't do him justice, Megan!' Helen reprimanded once the men were out of earshot. 'He is gorgeous, and the way he looks at you!'

'He does not.'

'Of course he does,' her friend insisted with a knowing laugh. 'Are you blind?'

Megan hesitated, feeling edgy and uncertain.

'If he does, if anyone does here, are they seeing me, or are they seeing Sophie?' she asked, voicing her disquiet aloud.

Before Helen could respond, Luke and Matt arrived back with the drinks, and they went to find a place to sit. Luke and Matt certainly seemed to have hit it off, Megan realised, listening to them talking easily about sport. This was the first time she had seen Luke away from the cottage. He seemed more relaxed and at ease, and proved to be attractive and funny in a much more natural and understated way than Dominic.

Helen, cuddled against Matt on a rustic bench, looking cosy and content, raised the question again of what Megan had planned.

'Have you given any more thought to working from home?' she asked.

'Kind of,' Megan replied. 'I heard from Mr Kaye this morning that some of the money is to be released this week and I'm planning to fix myself up with a decent computer system.'

'Is that what you do?' Luke asked, clearly interested.

'She's a whizz,' Helen confirmed with a grin.

Megan smiled.

'Hardly, but I have been thinking of starting my own web design business. It's deciding how best to go about it, how to advertise for business, if there is a market.'

'You can design a website for me,' Luke announced surprising her.

'Really?'

'I've been thinking about it for a while. I do use a computer for some of my garden layouts and designs, although I still prefer to do much of the work by hand. It would be good to be online properly, to be able to advertise my work to a wider client base.'

Helen looked delighted, as if this was all her own doing.

'Excellent! You see, Megan, and once you get started, it will spread by word of mouth.'

'There are several small businesses locally who could well be interested,' Luke added with unusual enthusiasm. 'People who do mail order and such like who could well be pleased to expand their reach.'

Feeling more confident about the idea, Megan resolved to give the idea a great deal of thought the following week and to work out a proper business plan.

Helping themselves to food, they sat round the table, relaxed and enjoying themselves, talking easily together. They had finished eating, lingering over their drinks, when Megan felt Luke stiffen and edge away from her.

'Great,' he muttered under his

breath. 'What is he doing here?'

Curious, Megan followed his gaze. 'What is it?'

'Dominic Brown. You haven't met.'

'They have!' Helen intervened mischievously, apparently unaware of the tension. 'They've been out to dinner.'

Luke's eyes darkened to narrowed slits.

'You went out with Dominic?'

'Yes,' Megan confirmed, confused at the anger in Luke's voice, cross she should feel the need to justify herself. 'Why?'

'Forget it.'

He turned to Matt and Helen.

'It was nice meeting you. Enjoy the rest of your evening.'

Then he was gone, disappearing into the crowd as Dominic spotted her and approached the table. Luke's behaviour had unsettled her. Why was he so angry? What was this thing between him and Dominic? Was there indeed something in Luke's past that he was hiding?

10

Luke walked home, a sour taste in his mouth. It had been typical of Dominic to show up and ruin things. He certainly hadn't wasted any time in running Megan to ground. Banging the front door angrily behind him, Luke tossed his keys on the table and went in search of a drink.

When had they met, he wondered, realising that it must have been Dominic whom Megan had been expecting the previous evening when he had called. How stupid of him not to have foreseen this possibility. But what could he do? There was no way he could compete with the sophistication and charm of Dominic Brown. He was nothing but a glorified gardener, for goodness' sake, and one with a past, to boot.

Tugga jumped on to his lap, her

purring warmth easing some of his tension. There was nothing he could do but allow events to run their course, he decided eventually, his expression grim. Nothing for it but to sit back and hope that Sophie knew what she was doing.

Meanwhile, Dominic, all smiles and charm, joined the others at the table, but for Megan at least, the joy had gone from the evening.

She was relieved when Helen suggested they went home, and she accepted the excuse to escape and leave Dominic behind.

'What was all that about?' Matt asked as they walked back to the cottage.

'I don't know,' Megan said with a frown.

Helen had her own ideas.

'Male rivalry.'

Matt raised an eyebrow.

'There's certainly no love lost between those two over something.'

'It must be to do with Sophie,' Megan decided.

'Whatever it is, Megan, I don't like

Dominic. He's shifty and false. Good looking, I grant you, but in a manufactured kind of way. Luke is more complex but a much more genuine character,' Helen announced.

Opening the door of the cottage, Megan laughed.

'You've only met them both for a short time.'

'Trust me. Remember Stuart.'

Helen's words rang in Megan's mind long after her friends had left for London the next afternoon. Trust — that was the problem. She just didn't know whom to trust, Luke or Dominic, or neither. She needed guidance from Sophie, but the only way she might find that was to locate the secret drawer.

Sitting in front of the bureau once more, Megan ran her fingers over the interior, searching for any sign of movement. She frowned. Was she on the wrong track entirely? Absently, she fiddled with an ornate knob at one corner, staring when it shifted in her hand. Had she broken it?

No, it definitely moved smoothly! Amazed at her discovery, she heard a click and a small panel edged aside. Sliding it across, Megan realised she had found the secret drawer at last!

She withdrew the hidden compartment, experiencing a dart of initial disappointment when she discovered nothing more exciting than a fat, leather-bound book. But on opening the cover, she found a folded sheet of paper.

Dear Megan,

I expect you are wondering why the subterfuge and the treasure hunt, but I didn't want all my most personal things left lying around for anyone to find. I began this diary ages ago but I never kept it up regularly, until, that is, I discovered my father's cache of old papers, letters and photographs, and found out about you for the first time.

The diary will explain more to you. Read it from the beginning, Megan, and once you have understood the family history and my life here, I hope you will come to understand and accept what I have left you. I may be wrong. I cannot explain what I feel. You may be married with half a dozen children, blissfully happy, not wanting any of this, and thinking I'm a raving old bat! But if you are not, and if you have questions of trust and friendship, and love, in your own life, then I hope this helps you to find some answers.

This is the last thing I can do, the rest is up to you. Now read on.

Sophie.

The first part of the diary was fragmented, Megan discovered, as she curled up on the settee in the living-room, the book in her hands. There were bits about Sophie's early life, memories of an austere and repressed father, a dominating mother, and a childhood spent alone. These were echoes of her own early years, Megan admitted, reliving, through Sophie's words, her difficult upbringing and sense of aloneness.

Perhaps these experiences had led to her own independence and self-reliance, just as they had for Sophie. Her aunt had clearly been determined to succeed, and in journalism she had found her niche. Having read some of her work she had discovered on the bookshelves, Megan already knew that Sophie had been an excellent writer, incisive, full of insight, direct, yet compassionate, too.

Impatient to read on and reach the parts about the family papers, Megan lingered long into the night over the first section of the diary. After a gap of some weeks, and a blank page, she found the next entry.

December 17.
I was amazed to find a box of Father's in the attic. I didn't even know I had it! It was well packed and hidden, but the contents were stunning, all manner of papers, letters and photographs I have never seen before. He

never talked of the family who disowned him, and I never knew until today that I had a half-sister, let alone a niece.

Megan, the niece, is about ten years younger than me. There are a couple of photos of her as a child, and I was shocked how much she looks like me, or did at that age. And it's not only the physical resemblance, but the attitude, the loneliness, the unhappiness in her eyes. What is it about this family that seems so unable to give any kind of affection, love or understanding?

Megan looked thoughtfully over the entry, realising that Sophie had indeed seen in those early photos exactly what she had been feeling, what she had always felt, all her life — excluded, unloved, alone. How sad that Sophie had felt the same.

Turning the page, Megan read the next entry.

December 20.

I can't stop thinking about Megan. I wish I knew where to find her, but there is no information so far, not even obsolete addresses. I wonder where she is now, what she is doing. Is she happy? I really need to know. I cannot begin to explain why I already feel a bond with someone I have never met. It sounds crazy, but I do. I thought I was the only one left of the family but clearly I am not. I have made up my mind. I am going to search for Megan.

Megan felt so many mixed emotions as she read Sophie's diary. There was warmth and pleasure that this woman had cared enough, felt enough, to want to trace her. Underlying that was an intense sadness that the search had only succeeded when it had been too late.

What had happened in those intervening weeks and months? Clearly Sophie had been well in December. She gave no hint of urgency or hidden agendas.

As tempted as she was to stay up and

read the diary from cover to cover, something held her back. She didn't want to spoil it. Sophie had intended her to take her time, to come to know the events of the past and to understand the present. Megan wanted to honour those wishes.

Time, thanks to Sophie, she now had, and time she would take, to uncover the secrets of her legacy.

★ ★ ★

Megan frowned at the shrilling telephone, annoyed at the interruption. She had just sat down next day to read another instalment of Sophie's diary, and now this. Rising gracefully to her feet, she crossed the room to answer the call.

'Hello?'

'Miss Fitzgerald, good to speak with you. It's Mr Kaye, here.'

'Oh, Mr Kaye!'

She smiled, genuine warmth stripping the irritation from her voice.

'How are you?'

'Fine, fine, thank you. And you? You are settling in?'

'Yes. I'm enjoying being here very much,' she confirmed, refraining from raising her simmering concerns about Luke and Dominic.

'Excellent.'

A rustle of paper followed and then his voice returned, more formal than before.

'Now, my dear, I have some papers for you to sign and I am also able to release some money for you. Are you able to call in to the office to see me?'

'Of course. When did you have in mind?'

'As soon as possible. No need for a fixed appointment.'

Megan looked towards the bureau where the diary lay and smothered a small sigh. This was equally important. The opportunity to access extra funds would be welcome and besides, Mr Kaye had been so kind to her.

'Would today be all right?' she asked.

'I do have some shopping I'd like to do, so I can take care of that at the same time.'

'That would be most convenient! Later this morning?'

'I'll look forward to seeing you.'

Megan locked the diary back in the bureau and went upstairs to change. After checking the house, conscious that another early morning had passed with no sign of Luke in the garden, she eased the car out of the driveway into the narrow lane and headed through the village towards Brighton.

It was the first time she had made the journey but she found her way to Mr Kaye's office without problems. Little more than an hour after she had spoken to him on the phone, she was crossing the reception area and smiling a greeting at the grim-faced Mrs Davies.

'It's Miss Fitzgerald, isn't it?' the older woman acknowledged with the barest softening of her expression. 'Please take a seat and I'll let Mr Kaye know you are here.'

'Thanks.'

She did not have to wait long before she was shown once more up the flight of stairs and along the corridor to Mr Kaye's office. He rose to greet her with a broad, warm smile, his handshake as strong and reassuring as ever.

'Well, now,' he began, his glasses once again perched on the bridge of his nose. 'How nice to see you again. I have to say you are looking very well.'

'I think the country air is agreeing with me.'

Megan smiled, touched by his kindly words.

'Indeed. Sorry to have asked you to come down at such short notice but I did think you would want to have these matters attended to as soon as possible.'

Megan watched as he slid a file from a stack beside him. Mr Kaye took some papers from it and began explaining them to her, clearing a small space as he passed them across for her signature.

'I think it should all be self-explanatory. It's more a matter of procedure and tying up loose ends.'

'That's fine, I quite understand,' Megan confirmed, scanning through the papers and signing them in her neat hand.

He took them back and closed the file.

'All done, for now anyway! I expect you would like to know when you can have some money.'

Megan hesitated, feeling uncomfortable about seeming too grasping.

'It's nothing for you to feel bad about. That is why we are here, after all, and you have to take care of yourself.'

Megan nodded, surprised that she cared so much what opinion Mr Kaye formed of her. As someone who had known and been close to Sophie, she did not want him to think she was frittering away her inheritance.

'I was hoping to set myself up to work from home. I have a technology degree and had just been made redundant from my job as a web designer when your letter arrived,' she explained. 'I've always wanted to branch out on my own but never expected to have the opportunity. I hope Sophie would have thought it a worthwhile use of my inheritance.'

'Sophie was a champion of personal enterprise, and she believed in people following their dreams and making a start for themselves. I cannot think of a better plan for you, my dear. Sophie would have supported you whole-heartedly.'

Mr Kaye's endorsement filled her with enthusiasm, gratitude and a burning desire to get started, to not let Sophie, or Mr Kaye, down.

'I'll need some expensive computer equipment and things, not to mention advertising and trying to get this off the ground,' she continued, voicing her requirements aloud, some anxiety evident in her tone at what lay ahead.

'I'm sure you will make a great success of it, and there is no time like the present! I suggest you take heart from the fact that your bank account is

133

now healthily in the black and go and make a start getting what you need.'

Megan rose to her feet, her own smile happy and excited.

'I will! Thank you.'

'I'll be in touch when there is any more business that needs attending to about the estate.'

Shaking her hand, Mr Kaye escorted her to the door.

'And do let me know how you are getting on.'

Carried along on a tide of upbeat enthusiasm, it was some while before she realised that she had never spoken to Mr Kaye about her concerns and asked his opinion of Luke and Dominic. Frowning, Megan determined to banish the thoughts that threatened to dampen her excitement and enjoyment. There would be time later to ponder her situation. For now, she had work to do!

11

Megan had never spent so much money in one go! She looked at the boxes and bags crammed in the back of her car and could not stifle a guilty giggle. When she had gone to the computer centre to explore what she would need, she had never expected to have found all she wanted straight away, let alone to have bought and paid for it.

'Well,' she muttered to herself as she opened the front door and attempted to manoeuvre the first of the heavy boxes into the cottage, 'Mr Kaye did tell me to go for it!'

She left the first box in the study and was returning to the open front door when she heard the sound of a vehicle pulling up behind hers in the drive. Wondering who it could be, she stepped outside, feeling a shiver of alarm and awareness as Luke closed the door of his van and came to meet her.

'Megan.'

'Hello,' she acknowledged him.

They faced each other in silence for a moment, tension crackling between them, then Luke glanced towards her car, releasing her from the spell of his gaze.

'Are these going indoors?'

'Yes.'

'Let me help you.'

Luke lifted the heaviest box of computer equipment as if it were no more than a matchbox. Thankful for his help, but nervous of his presence, Megan went ahead to show him where she wanted her new possessions. Feeling skittish and awkward, she left him in the study and went back to the car for another load. They met in the front doorway. Megan stumbled and nearly dropped her printer as she bumped into his solid, unnerving frame.

'Steady,' Luke chastised, his hands

reaching out to balance and protect her. 'You OK?'

Megan found herself far too close to him. Her gaze clashed with his. His grey eyes darkened as he looked down at her, and her own widened with unchecked alarm as, for an instant, he held her closer. Moistening dry lips with the tip of her tongue, Megan forced herself to step away from him.

'I'm fine,' she stressed, her voice unaccountably husky.

She hurried to the study, drawing in a deep and steadying breath. This was ridiculous! What was it about the man that had her in such a tizzy? Was it her doubts about him and his shady past, or was it the fiery effect he seemed to have on her well-being?

'This is the last of them.'

Luke's voice made her jump and she turned to see him place the last of the boxes on the floor.

'Thanks for your help.'

'My pleasure. You're going to set up on your own then?'

'Yes. I spoke about it with Mr Kaye. He seemed to support the idea.'

'Sophie would have approved, too.'

'Thank you. I hope so.'

Their gazes met again, his grey and intense and revealing nothing of his feelings. Megan shifted uneasily, clasping her hands together in front of her.

'Do you want some help unpacking this stuff?' Luke asked.

'I think I can manage.'

He nodded, his gaze straying towards the window.

'My afternoon appointment called to reschedule, so I thought I'd spend some time in the garden. That OK with you?'

'Yes,' she acknowledged, summoning a smile. 'Of course. Thank you.'

'I'll get on then. Let me know if you need any help.'

He was gone. Megan heard the front door click shut and expelled a shaky breath. She realised she had skipped lunch, so she went through to the kitchen to make a sandwich and drink before busying herself making a start on assembling her new computer system, anything to take her mind off Luke's presence outside.

It took a while, but Megan eventually had everything up and running. She sat back, looking at her new work area and sophisticated system with a mix of pride, anticipation and excitement. Her next job would be to design a website for herself, advertising her services and showing what she could do. All she would need then would be clients! It was a daunting thought, but one which filled her with a sense of challenge, too. She was determined her venture would be a success.

Stifling a yawn, she went through to the kitchen and put the kettle on for a well-earned cup of tea. She glanced out of the window while she waited, surprised to see Luke walking up the path carrying some empty pots in one hand, a muddied fork and spade in the other.

Goodness, he was still here! Megan ignored the dart of unease that fluttered in her chest. She watched as Luke cleaned the garden tools at the outside tap, forcing herself to cross the kitchen as he propped them against the wall and tapped on the door.

'I'm just finishing up for the day.'

'OK. Thanks.'

He looked hot, she realised, seeing the beads of perspiration on his face. The sound of the kettle clicking on the boil penetrated the silence. Megan glanced round, then back at him, and cleared her throat.

'I was just making some tea. Would you care for a cup, or something cold?'

'Something cold would be welcome.'

Unable to avoid it, Megan invited him in.

'I have ginger beer, diet Coke, or fruit juice.'

'Ginger beer sounds good. OK if I wash up?'

'Of course,' Megan allowed, gesturing towards the sink.

She found a glass and poured out the

ice cold drink, setting it on the table before making her own tea. All the time she was aware of Luke watching her. A tingle ran up her spine at his almost brooding speculation.

'Have you managed to set up all your computer stuff?' he asked as she sat down at the table opposite him.

'Yes, thanks. I'm all ready to go.'

'What's the first step?'

'I was just pondering that myself,' she admitted with a smile. 'I was thinking of doing my own website first to advertise and display my work. Then I'll need customers. Sounds easy, doesn't it?'

His own expression softened at the self-mockery in her tone.

'No, not easy. It never is, not if it's worth it, but hard work brings its own rewards.'

'Let's hope so.'

'I was serious about you designing a site for me,' he went on, taking a draught of his own drink. 'When you're ready, let me know.'

'I will. Thanks, Luke.'

Silence settled again, more comfortable this time, and Megan found herself watching his work-roughened hands as they cradled the icy glass, remembering their feel on her skin when he had steadied her stumble earlier that afternoon. Her gaze returned to his face to find him studying her. She bit her lip, wanting to clear the air between them but unsure what to say.

'Luke, about the other night at the pub.'

'You don't have to explain anything to me,' he responded coolly.

'No, I know, but . . . '

'Forget it, Megan.'

The angry look in his eyes and the sternness of his voice made her pause. Why was it so hard to talk to him? Why could she never come to know him, to understand, to unravel just what was going on between him and Dominic, and how the pair of them were connected to Sophie?

Before she could continue the conversation, Luke rose to his feet.

'Thanks for the drink.'

She nodded, feeling troubled and uneasy once more. Luke placed his glass in the sink and walked to the door. He hesitated, glancing back at her as if he wanted to say something, then shook his head.

'What is it?' she asked.

'Nothing,' he replied and his weak smile failed to strip the frown from his face. 'Good luck with your venture, Megan.'

Megan puzzled over his reaction and his words long after he had gone. It was all so unsettling. She wished she understood what was going on.

After sending a few e-mails to friends, including a long one to Helen, she made herself a salad, fetched Sophie's diary from its hiding place, and went outside to relax in the warm evening stillness.

The diary entries immediately after Sophie's announcement that she intended to search for Megan related mostly to investigations of the family history, Megan discovered. An entry at New Year revealed the search had been initiated but so far was unsuccessful. Sophie's disappointment was tangible. Then there was a break and there were no more entries until February and Megan was startled at the change in tone.

February 5.
I've been feeling poorly for a few weeks now but ignored it. Now I can't ignore it any more. Tests show I am ill, really ill. I feel numb with shock and can't take it in. I want to talk, need to, and yet I can't, at least not with Dominic.

February 8.
I knew Dominic would have little patience with illness. It was my mistake to mention it, but he has proved me right. Thank goodness for Luke. What would I do without him?

Megan was surprised at this first diary mention of both the men who were causing her such heart-searching. What rôles had they played in Sophie's life? Eager to discover more, she read on.

February 10.
The answer to my last question is that I clearly don't have to. I should have known. Luke has been fantastic. He listens, he understands, and he is even helping me search for Megan. It's a search that now seems even more important. If I feel OK tomorrow Luke is taking me to town to see Mr Kaye so I can put my affairs in order. I know Luke is upset, and I also know what Dominic thinks, but I refuse to be ostrich-like about it. I intend to make sure there are no doubts about my wishes.

February 14.
Some Valentine's Day! Dominic came with flowers and chocolates and

charming apologies. Why can I never resist him? At least I didn't tell him the consequences of my visit to Mr Kaye! Dominic has his own opinions and needs, and they do not always coincide with mine. I think he will be in for a shock!

Again Megan paused in her reading, a frown on her face as she tried to decipher the hidden messages in Sophie's words. Clearly Luke was a friend to her, someone she trusted, but Dominic was something more. There was a deeper relationship there. So why was Sophie cautious? What exactly was she keeping from Dominic and why?

'Yoo-hoo! Miss Fitzgerald? Are you there, dear?'

The persistent voice snapped Megan from her thoughts. She rose from her chair on the patio in time to see Mabel Atkins come round the side of the house. Hastily, Megan slipped Sophie's diary behind a cushion.

'So sorry to disturb you, Megan. May

I call you Megan?' Mabel enquired, hastening on before Megan could respond. 'I've been wondering how you are getting on.'

'Very well, thank you.'

'I'm so glad. We were all so upset about dear Sophie. Having you here makes the cottage feel less lonely. Her spirit lives on here.'

Megan managed a polite smile.

'Yes.'

'Now, I'm having a small event at my house at the weekend and I do hope you will attend. It will be an opportunity for you to meet more people. I gather you have become quite friendly with Catherine. She'll be coming over so it won't all be strangers!'

'That's very kind of you. I'll see how I'm fixed.'

Mabel looked disappointed at the lukewarm response but rallied.

'I would so like to involve you in village affairs. I chair quite a few committees and things and I'm sure we could find something that would interest you. New blood is always welcome.'

'I expect so,' Megan murmured. 'I'm just setting up my own business so I'm not sure if I'll have time for anything else at the moment.'

'Really? How exciting! In what, dear?' Mabel enquired, her eyes sparkling as she sensed some first-hand gossip to pass around the village.

Megan hid a smile and explained her venture.

'Very clever, I'm sure,' Mabel said. 'I'm afraid I am not very well up on computers.'

'I'm sure you are very well up in many other things, Mabel.'

'Indeed! I mustn't keep you. Do think about joining us on Saturday.'

'Thank you, I will.'

Megan sighed with relief as the rotund form disappeared back the way it had come. Rescuing the diary, she went back inside the house, hoping for no more interruptions.

She checked her e-mails, smiling

when she found a wordy and light-hearted response from Helen. She sped a note back, telling her about Mabel's visit and a bit about the diary, then logged off, intending to spend the rest of the evening reading the diary. However, the telephone thwarted her good intentions.

'Megan,' Dominic's voice purred, 'I've been trying to reach you today.'

'I've been out, then busy on the computer,' Megan allowed, unable to banish all stiffness from her tone.

'I was hoping you'd come out to dinner with me again this week.'

'I'm very busy at the moment,' she said, not at all sure she wanted to be alone with Dominic again until she had unravelled what was going on.

'I really want to see you. Perhaps I could bring something round and spend some time with you.'

'Maybe another time, Dominic.'

'I suppose it's Luke Warrender, is it?'

Megan frowned at the venom and petulance in Dominic's voice.

'I beg your pardon? What has Luke to do with anything?'

'You tell me. He's sniffing around there, isn't he, around you, just as he did with Sophie?'

'I have no idea what you are talking about, nor do I intend to have this conversation with you,' she said, shocked by Dominic's change from charmer to accuser. 'It is best if you don't call or try to see me again.'

A tense silence followed. When he spoke again, his voice was harsh with menace and intent.

'No-one is going to take what is mine a second time, do you understand, Megan? This isn't over.'

12

'He said what?' Helen exclaimed in disbelief after she'd listened to Megan's call, so Megan repeated her conversation with Dominic, still feeling shaky and indignant and confused.

'I'm still not sure what he was getting at.'

'He sounds crazy, Megan. I don't like to think of you there on your own.'

'Thanks,' she said wryly. 'Make me feel better, why don't you?'

'Sorry.'

'It's OK.'

'I hope you told him to get lost,' Helen continued angrily.

'Kind of, and I hung up on him.'

'Good. Do it again if he rings back, and don't open the door.'

'I'm sure he won't come round here,' Megan replied, trying to reassure herself as well as her friend.

'Ring me if you need anything.'

'I will. Talk to you or e-mail you tomorrow.'

After checking all the doors and windows were closed securely, Megan drew the curtains and curled up on the sofa with the diary. It had been quite a day and it was still only mid-evening.

What had Dominic been driving at, she wondered for the umpteenth time. He'd been so charming, too charming, but now he had changed suddenly. Why? What was he after? And where did Luke fit into it all?

Disturbed by Helen's concerns and the thought of Dominic trying to contact her again, Megan shook her head and vowed to finish the diary. Surely it must contain the final clues.

February 23, she read on.

Have had several days of feeling much better and I've been out with Dominic again. Luke warned me, but something keeps drawing me back like a moth to a flame. I know he is all surface charm and no substance. In fact, he is very self-obsessed, but I need to be romanced right now, to feel desirable again, even if I do know that Dominic is a fair-weather friend.

March 2.
My days of feeling well seem to be over. I know what lies ahead. Part of me feels quite resigned, quite calm, but another part of me is regretful about all the things I'll never do, and deep down I am angry and frightened. The illness has been hidden for so long and has progressed so quickly. They told me today there was nothing more they could do. It's just time, and I really want to find Megan. I am frustrated we have made so little progress. At least I have Luke.

March 6.
Megan, where are you? I think it is going to be too late and I'm not going to find you in time. Mr Kaye knows what to do. I've made up my mind. I

want Megan to be my main heir. About the only thing my father ever did for me was leave me financially provided for. As he was Megan's grandfather, I feel it is the least I can do. It's rightfully hers now.

At least I have finally seen Dominic for what he really is. He told me he had invested time in me, as if inheriting from me would be what he deserved! Well, he can think again! He will get nothing from me.

Megan sat back at this revelation. So Dominic had been a snake in the grass. He had simply been out for what he could get from Sophie, and now from her. Anger built inside her at the way he had deliberately sought her out and tried to smooth-talk his way into her life. All the time he had been trying to get something back he felt he had missed out on with Sophie. At least some things were starting to make sense.

The diary had been an emotional

read so far, but the next entries brought a painful lump to Megan's throat. Sophie's handwriting had deteriorated with each entry and was now harder to decipher, a poignant sign of her failing health.

March 11.
There's so much more that I want to write, to say, but I just don't seem to have the strength now. Megan, if you read this, know that I so wanted to meet you. I don't know why I feel so close to you. You'll probably think I am crazy, but it has meant so much to me to know you are there and trying to find you has given me a goal to carry on.

I may be wrong, but you'll still have the cottage and money to do with as you choose. No obligations, Megan. Stay or go, whatever you like, but if you decide to live here and bring life and laughter back to the place I have loved so much, Luke will be a friend to you. His story is his own to tell. All I can say is that he has an incredible capacity for caring. Despite, or maybe because of what he has been through, he is the most giving and loyal friend anyone could have. I entrust you to him, Megan, with my whole heart.

March 14.
So tired, Luke is here all the time now. He has been my rock, my support, easing me through every step of this journey that was not of my choosing. I worry so for him when I'm not here. I don't want him going into himself. He's done so well. If things work out as I hope, if you are found, Megan, and if you can enjoy the kind of friendship with Luke that I did, I will be happy. Whatever you decide, know you were loved by this member of the family.
I have organised things this way because I wanted you to live here and experience things rather than hear about them in the formality of a solicitor's office. Perhaps it will all mean more to you, the cottage, Luke,

everything, if you have lived in it for a while. It will be real.

Be happy, Megan, not sad. I have come to appreciate time, and opportunity. Live life to the full, follow your heart, reach for your dreams. I wish all this for you, and a long and wonderful life . . .

The diary ended abruptly here.

Tears spilled from Megan's eyes as she absorbed Sophie's final words. More than ever she wished that she had met this generous, loving woman. She felt a wave of guilt and sadness that she had stepped into Sophie's life, had inherited all this, because Sophie was gone. But that was the way Sophie had planned it, Megan acknowledged, wiping the salty tears from her cheeks. Sophie had wanted this, wanted for her to enjoy it, to live on.

Closing the diary, Megan hugged it to her chest. She sat for a moment, lost in thought, then looked at the precious book, running her fingers over the leather-bound cover with reverence and appreciation. Rising to her feet, she crossed to the bureau, tucking the precious book back into the secret compartment. Megan knew now what she needed to do.

13

Dusk was falling as Megan let herself out of the cottage. Her heart was heavy, yet filled with awe at Sophie's courage and generosity.

She walked along the deserted lanes to the village, her mind full of all she had read, of what Sophie had revealed. Reaching her destination, the tiny brick-built cottage at the end of a terrace set off the main village street, Megan found herself strangely nervous. She paused, her hand on the wrought-iron gate. Was she right to have come? What was she going to say? Was she just being swept along by emotion?

Light spilled from the curtained front window confirming the owner was in. All she had to do was walk up the path and ring the bell, simple. Annoyed at her lack of gumption, Megan stepped up to the door before she could change her mind. Her stomach knotted as she rang the bell and waited for an answer. Just as she was beginning to waver, the door opened, framing Luke in the light.

He had always made her nervous. She was so aware of him. When she hadn't known if she could trust him, she could blame her unease on lack of certainty. Now, with Sophie's endorsement and reassurance, she felt more, not less, edgy and tense.

'Megan,' he greeted her in surprise, his expression guarded. 'Is everything OK?'

'Yes. Yes, fine,' she stammered.

'Do you want to come in?'

'Is that all right? I know it's late.'

'Of course it's OK.'

He stood aside for her and after closing the door, he showed her into a small but surprisingly cosy living-room, the walls plainly painted but hung with bright, pleasing landscapes.

'Please, sit down,' he invited.

Megan did as she was bid, suddenly tongue-tied and wondering why she had been so compelled to come here. Really, she knew why, just wasn't sure if it was sensible to have acted on it.

'Can I get you something to drink?' Luke offered.

'Whatever you're having, thank you.'

'I'll open some wine.'

As he disappeared from the room, Megan expelled a shaky breath. His magnetism was frightening. She tried to quell her nerves by glancing round the room. There were plenty of books cramming the shelves in alcoves either side of a narrow fireplace, novels and she could see Sophie's books, biographies, wildlife and conservation, archaeology books, along with a couple of shelves devoted to gardening and plants.

The room also contained a television, comfortable but mismatched chairs, and a mini hi-fi with a rack full of CDs nearby. Aside from the paintings on the walls there were no adornments, no photographs.

She still knew so little about this

enigmatic, secretive man.

Meanwhile, Luke lingered in the kitchen. Why had she come? He felt as if he had been treading on egg shells around her these last days. They had seemed to be getting to know one another but always Megan was wary, backing off from him. Then something had changed and the wariness in her eyes had been replaced by a genuine alarm that had hit him hard.

Had someone been saying things to her? Dominic? He wrestled with the corkscrew and smothered a curse. If only he knew what was going on, and what Sophie had planned, but now Megan was here and something had changed. He thought she had been crying. Her eyes had looked bruised, like crushed leaves, but behind the lingering emotion was a different sort of wariness, a new understanding and openness. Hope stirred inside him.

Luke poured the wine and picked up the glasses, hesitating in the doorway to watch her for a moment, undetected.

She was so beautiful. From the first moment, she had slipped under his skin and given him no peace. He had never been much good with people, and his social life had been non-existent since Sophie had become ill.

For the first time since her loss, he felt renewed excitement and zest burgeoning within him. That was due to Megan. He felt like something had been hibernating and was now coming out of a long sleep and being restored to the full bloom of life.

Tugga miaowed, brushing against his legs as she pushed past him in the doorway, drawing Megan's attention. Pulling himself together, Luke controlled his thoughts and walked towards her.

Megan smiled as the cat crossed to her and rubbed against her legs with sinuous grace before jumping up on to the settee and settling against her.

'I seem to have made a friend,' she ventured as Luke handed her a glass of red wine. 'Thanks for this. What's your cat's name?'

'Tugga.'

Megan looked up at him question-ingly.

'When she was a kitten she'd tug everything out of cupboards, off tables or the bed,' he informed her with a shy smile. 'The name just stuck.'

'She's gorgeous. Where did you get her?'

'I found her. A litter of four was abandoned by the woods when they were only two or three weeks old. She was the only one to make it.'

As Luke sat in the chair opposite her, his gaze on her, Megan stroked the warm, purring body, affected by the anger and tenderness that mingled in Luke's voice, upset herself that anyone should be so cruel as to leave any creatures to die. She imagined him saving the tiny animals, sad when one after another was lost, determined to keep going, nursing Tugga to life.

'Why have you come, Megan?'

His directness gave her no time for

prevarication. She took a sip of her wine for much-needed courage, her gaze flitting to his and away again.

'I don't know how much you are aware of what Sophie left for me,' she began, a frown on her face at her stumbling, awkward explanations. 'I don't mean in terms of money, or the cottage, but other things, personal things.'

She looked across at him.

'It was you who tied the envelope on the statue, wasn't it?'

'Yes.'

'Do you know why?'

'Because Sophie asked me to,' he responded simply. 'If you came, if you stayed, she wanted me to post you a letter and then leave the other one at the statue.'

'Did she tell you about the family things, the diary?'

It was Luke's turn to frown.

'I knew Sophie was safeguarding papers and photographs. She didn't want anyone but you to have them. I don't know anything about a diary.'

'It was the last piece of the puzzle,' she explained. 'She wrote it for me, telling me about her search, her illness.'

Megan hesitated, wondering how to continue with what she wanted to say. Luke didn't make it easy for her, regarding her with that silent, watchful stillness. She cleared her throat and took another sip of her drink.

'Sophie made it abundantly clear what you meant to her, Luke,' she went on, her voice soft, watching the emotion in his eyes at her words. 'You stayed with her until the end, made everything so much more bearable for her. I want to thank you for that.'

'You don't have to thank me.'

His voice gruff, Luke rose to his feet and crossed the room, staring out at the blackness of the moonless night. Giving him time, needing still to explain, Megan concentrated on the purring animal beside her, as if telling the cat was easier than telling Luke.

'I didn't understand at first, not only

why Sophie would leave anything to me when I was a stranger to her, but why she had arranged the mysterious hunt and clues. But I think I realise now that she wanted me to get to know this place, and the people, especially you, before I formed any judgements or made any decisions. It's hard, Luke,' she went on, as he maintained his distant, watchful silence. 'I feel guilty that I've stepped into Sophie's life and she isn't here, and yet privileged and honoured that she's not only given me a family history I didn't know I had, but these chances for security, too.'

'Sophie wouldn't want you to feel guilty.'

Luke turned from the darkened window and stared at her. He re-crossed the room, but instead of returning to his chair, he came to sit beside her on the settee.

'I didn't know how much to tell you. You're right. Sophie wanted you to reach your own conclusions,' he admitted, finishing his glass of wine.

'Searching for you became so important for her. I understood that. But she had this ideal image of what she imagined you to be.'

'And I may not have lived up to her expectations,' she finished for him.

He smiled then in genuine amusement.

'I think Sophie would have been more than delighted, Megan, if she had known you.'

'Thanks.'

A tinge of colour stained her cheeks. High praise from Luke, indeed!

'Then what did you mean?'

'Just that you may have been uninterested, may not have wanted to meet her, and afterwards, perhaps you would have wanted to sell up and move on. You may have been happily settled elsewhere with a family of your own, or you may never have been found.'

'I understand.'

'The way she planned it meant that you would only have discovered the real Sophie, and all she wanted you to know, if you were the kind of person she hoped you would be.'

Megan mulled over what Luke had said, filling in the few remaining gaps for herself. What she still didn't know was his own story. Where had he fitted in? There had clearly been a bond between them, but just how had Luke felt about Sophie? Cradling her glass in one hand, and stroking the cat with the other, Megan frowned, concerned that it suddenly mattered to her just what Luke's feelings really were.

Why did it bother her so intensely? How had she come to care so much about this complex, secretive and self-contained man? She was scared what his answer might be, but she had to ask the question uppermost in her mind.

'You must have loved Sophie very much.'

'Yes,' Luke admitted, his voice gruff. 'Yes, I loved her. I always will.'

Megan felt a crushing, bitter disappointment. How could she have expected any less? She chastised herself. Could she ever have imagined that Luke would look at her and see her for herself, not some image of Sophie? Hadn't she learned that lesson with Dominic?

'Of course. I knew really.'

She pressed a hand to her chest, as if by doing so she could ease the knot of pain that grew there.

'I don't think you do.'

Surprised at the serious tone of his voice, Megan glanced at him.

'I loved Sophie, but not in a romantic way,' he explained, holding her gaze. 'I loved her as a big sister, best friend, as the only person who had ever cared about me or shown me any understanding or affection.'

Megan was intrigued that while outwardly aloof and independent, Luke had revealed a vulnerable core.

'How did you and Sophie meet?'

For a moment, Megan wondered if he would answer her. But he took a sip of his wine and sat back.

'She found me, really. I was seventeen, a typical angry young man. Sophie was working on a story about kids who had gone through the care system and what happened to them afterwards.'

'And had you?' she prompted when he hesitated. 'Been through care, I mean?'

'If you can call it care,' he responded with a mirthless laugh.

'What happened?'

'I won't give you the gory details, just know that it was pretty rough. Loveless, no sense of purpose, hope or belonging.'

The hurt and loneliness in his voice brought an answering ache inside her.

'And then you met Sophie?'

'Yes. I'd been in trouble with the police, pretty minor stuff, but I could have gone either way at that point. If not for Sophie, I don't know where I would be today. She saw something in me I didn't know was there and took me in hand.'

He looked up, smiling at the memory.

'She pushed me to make something of myself, and for the first time in my life, she showed me what it was to love and be loved, to have someone believe in you. I responded to the attention and understanding like a starving man devouring food. She helped me get on a training course, encouraged me to work hard at the one thing I enjoyed, and here I am, ten years later, on my feet and with my own business.'

'You've done brilliantly.'

'Everything I have become is thanks to Sophie. She rescued me, Megan, and a lot of other people were not so lucky. I'll never forget what she did for me. She gave me so much more in life than I can ever explain or repay.'

'I can't imagine Sophie wanted any repayment,' Megan was moved to comment, touched by the image of the lonely, vulnerable and unloved youngster Sophie had taken under her wing.

Unable to stop herself, she reached

out to touch his hand.

'I think the way you have turned out and everything that you gave her in friendship was ample reward. She cared about you so much, and was so proud of you, Luke.'

Luke moved his hand under hers, turning it so that he could link their fingers. The touch sent a shiver of awareness through her. Her gaze clashed with his, seeing the empathy, the understanding, the attraction in the grey depths. When his free hand rose to brush the fall of hair back from her face, her heart started to thud against her ribs and time seemed to stand still.

'Luke . . . '

'I was fascinated by you the first moment I laid eyes on you,' he told her, his voice husky and warm. 'But you were so wary and kept backing off.'

'I wasn't sure if you just saw Sophie in me.'

He shook his head.

'There is a family likeness, of course, but you are your own person, Megan. I do not think of Sophie when I look at you.'

Flustered, Megan wanted everything out in the open.

'Then there was Dominic,' she admitted, disappointed at Luke's partial retreat at the mention of the other man's name.

'How could I forget?'

'He's nothing, Luke, not to Sophie, not to me.'

'You went out with him.'

'Just once. I was nearly taken in by that surface charm, and he made such an effort to meet me, to be with me. He saw me as some kind of substitute for her, but I know him now for what he is. I know what he did to Sophie. He tried so hard to sow seeds of doubt in my mind about whom I should trust, who had been close to Sophie, but he's just after what he feels he has lost. Dominic doesn't matter, Luke. I want nothing to do with him.'

Whatever lingering doubts had been in Luke's mind appeared to have been eased by her anger, Megan realised, as his eyes were clear of wariness and concern when he looked back at her.

'He was no good for her, but Sophie had a mind of her own.'

'You were there to pick up the pieces.'

'I tried to be. I owed her so much more than that.'

'You were there, Luke, always,' Megan stressed, wanting to make him see. 'That's what love really means.'

'I still can't believe she's gone.'

'I know. I so wish I had known her, too.'

'I still feel the need to tell her something, or I see something I want to share with her, and then I realise that I can't.'

Tears stung her eyes at the emotion in Luke's simple, heartfelt words.

'I'm sorry.'

'Don't waste time on sadness, that's what Sophie always said.'

With a gentle smile, he brushed away the moisture on her cheek.

'I meant what I said, Megan. Sophie would be so glad you are here, that you are everything and more than she hoped you would be.'

'Oh, Luke!'

'There will always be an ache of loss, but my memories are happy ones. Sophie's legacy to me was one of love and hope. I'll never forget that.'

Megan nodded, unable to steady her voice, touched by the gentle strength of this surprisingly caring and intuitive man. Sophie had been so right about him. Her faith in Luke had not been misplaced.

'Sophie's hopes and dreams have brought you here, Megan.'

'Yes,' she allowed, thinking back to the day she had first discovered her inheritance. 'And I was in such a rut in my life, Luke. I'd been made redundant, I'd lost my flat, and I had just escaped from a bad relationship. I'd give anything for Sophie still to be here, but she gave me a new chance at life.'

Luke's fingers tightened round hers

in supportive understanding.

'She lives on in us. We both have a chance to find happiness now.'

As his words sunk in, Megan wondered if Sophie could possibly have sensed that her unknown niece and this lonely, loving man, needed each other. It sounded far-fetched, but whether by chance or by destiny, Sophie's legacy for them both was more precious than any material things.

Smiling through her tears, they moved towards each other. Luke's first kiss was tentative, but as she met and matched the caress, welcoming the flare of excitement and fierce, needy desire that deepened between them, Megan knew this was a legacy they could explore together, a legacy that would grow between them.

Held in Luke's arms, feeling protected and loved and cherished, Megan could think of nowhere else she ever wanted to be. Together they would share their dreams at Honeysuckle Cottage, and with all that Sophie's love and generosity had bestowed upon them — and they would never forget.

Theirs was an unexpected legacy of love and hope for the future.

THE END